DUE TO A DEATH

DUE TO A DEATH

MARY KELLY

With an Introduction
by Martin Edwards

Published by Poisoned Pen Press, an imprint of Sourcebooks, in association with the British Library
P.O. Box 4410, Naperville, Illinois 60567-4410
(630) 961-3900
sourcebooks.com

Due to a Death was originally published in 1962 by Michael Joseph, London, UK.

Library of Congress Cataloging-in-Publication Data

Names: Kelly, Mary, author. | Edwards, Martin, writer of introduction.
Title: Due to a death / Mary Kelly ; with an introduction by Martin Edwards.
Description: Naperville, Illinois : Poisoned Pen Press, [2022] | Series: British Library crime classics | Due to a death is also known in the U.S. as The dead of summer.
Identifiers: LCCN 2021023654 (print) | LCCN 2021023655 (ebook) | (trade paperback) | (epub)
Subjects: LCGFT: Detective and mystery fiction. | Thrillers (Fiction). | Novels.
Classification: LCC PR6061.E495 D84 2022 (print) | LCC PR6061.E495 (ebook) | DDC 823/.914--dc23
LC record available at https://lccn.loc.gov/2021023654
LC ebook record available at https://lccn.loc.gov/2021023655

Printed and bound in the United States of America.
SB 10 9 8 7 6 5 4 3 2 1

CONTENTS

Introduction vii
Due to a Death 1

INTRODUCTION

Due to a Death, known in the U.S. as *The Dead of Summer,* was first published just as Mary Kelly's fame reached its peak. The year was 1962, and she'd recently won the coveted Gold Dagger for best crime novel, awarded by the Crime Writers' Association, for *The Spoilt Kill.* She'd pipped such distinguished authors as John Le Carré to the prize.

Many novelists would have been tempted to cash in on this success and produce a highly commercial follow-up. Instead, although Kelly did bring back Hedley Nicholson, the private investigator who narrated *The Spoilt Kill* (also republished by Poisoned Pen Press, in association with the British Library), this time he is seen from an entirely different perspective. This enigmatic mystery is unorthodox and very, very far from cosy. But while some critics were nonplussed, again the book was in contention for the Gold Dagger, although this time the award went to Joan Fleming.

The narrator of *Due to a Death* is a young woman and as the story begins, she says it is: 'Thirty minutes since I'd run away.' Run away from what, from whom? She is wounded and bleeding and a passenger in a car which an unnamed man is driving wildly: 'A last mile at eighty-five with the police closing up behind, impatient, menacing.'

The bleak landscape in which these curious events unfold is described evocatively and with an undercurrent of menace: 'there was nothing to be seen of the estuary; only...a wide marine sky embossed with pearly clouds, and the slow plumes of the cement works' chimneys...concrete posts and barbed wire half swamped by chalk-dusted thickets...a red rust-pitted disc: POLICE ADVICE—DANGER, KEEP OUT.'

It becomes clear that the police are not chasing the couple in the car, and the pair learn that a girl has been found dead on the marsh: 'dead, stripped and dumped.' As the first chapter draws to a close, the narrator seeks sanctuary in a church and contemplates the extraordinary summer that has led up to this moment: 'They could be tied together, after all, my own troubles and the girl on the marsh, one horror, worse than anything I'd ever known... I had to go back to the beginning; though there is never a beginning, only a point when you wake up.'

Thus the scene is set for a story told in flashback about the people of Gunfleet, one of those small places where everyone knows everyone else. It's the sort of closed community familiar from Golden Age whodunits, but this was a book—in the early 1960s—of a determinedly modern kind, with a strong focus on character and relationships. Agnes, the narrator, is married to a man called Tom, but she feels discontented with her life and finds herself drawn to a newcomer to the village—Nicholson. The melancholy mood is reinforced by Gunfleet's atmosphere of decay.

The darkness of *Due to a Death* represented a striking reaction to the success of *The Spoilt Kill*. Her publishers, Michael Joseph, had hailed Kelly as 'the new Dorothy L. Sayers,' but although she admired Sayers' writing, Kelly belonged to a younger generation, and as a crime novelist she had very different preoccupations and did not wish to be bracketed with authors of the Golden Age. *Due to a Death* was in no sense an autobiographical novel, and Agnes was not a self-portrait. Kelly felt driven to write the book because of the anger she'd felt when working in hospitals in the East End as an auxiliary nurse (to say more in this introduction would be a spoiler).

Mary Theresa Coolican was born in London in 1927, and studied at Edinburgh University; there she met a fellow student, Denis Kelly. They married, and became teachers. An experience while hitch-hiking from Edinburgh inspired her first novel. This was *A Cold Coming*, published in 1956, and the first of three novels featuring Inspector Brett Nightingale.

Kelly told a journalist who interviewed her after that Gold Dagger triumph that typically she started work on a book with 'vague and chaotic' thoughts, often inspired by a particular *milieu*. She and Denis were both keen botanists, and while looking for rare orchids in Kent, they discovered Greenhithe, in those days an almost-forgotten spot by the Thames. As Denis explained to me, they didn't find marsh helleborine, but Mary realized that she'd found the ideal location for her next novel. Greenhithe duly metamorphosed into Gunfleet.

Her usual method of writing a novel was to begin by filling a notebook with ideas and rough sketches of scenes. While researching *Due to a Death*, she stayed occasionally at the Bull & George, an old coaching inn at Dartford, taking inspiration from the fact that Jane Austen had once stopped off there too. On day trips by car, she and her husband sometimes took a break at a local pub, where Denis recalls the jukebox rocking constantly to the tune of Eden Kane, singing his number one hit 'Well I Ask You.'

After six months of preparation, her ideas crystallized so that she was ready to start writing in earnest. Denis read her day's output each evening, but when she reached the final stages of the book, she liked to go away to be on her own in order to complete the manuscript.

H. R. F. Keating said in *Twentieth Century Crime and Mystery Writers* of Kelly: 'Her writing is moment by moment intense, and successful as such. Whatever she has to describe, whether scene or action (or sexual relations, in the description of which—a difficult task—she is particularly good), she does so in a way that puts the reader there. Unusually for crime novels, therefore, what propels the reader through the pages is not the tug of "who done it" nor the excitement of men with guns coming through doors, but the sheer excellence of the writing.'

In an interview with a Dutch magazine in 1969, Kelly was asked whether she intended to continue to write detective stories, given that her work was frequently compared to Graham Greene's. Even in translation, there was no lack of clarity in her answer: 'I shall stick to this. This is just what I want. I love the discipline and order which this imposes. I should perhaps get lost in lack of form and all I want is a straight line… I want to grip people by the mystery and to have attention to the last page due to the unsolved secret so that they cannot leave it. That is what I want—to grip them and force them to read to the bitter end. That is why I try sometimes something new. In *Due to a Death* I first give a tantalizing view of the end without telling the secret…'

Nevertheless, after 1974 Kelly published no more novels. As a result, by the time of her death in 2017, she was almost forgotten by crime fans. The republication of several of her titles in the British Library Crime Classics series has led to a revival of interest that is as welcome as it is overdue. She was a talented novelist whose contribution to the crime genre was intriguing and distinctive.

—Martin Edwards
www.martinedwardsbooks.com

Chapter One

'I'M BRAKING,' HE SAID. 'HOLD ON.'

I pushed my fingers under my glasses and gave myself up to the pressure of the tightening belt. The car pulled left and dragged to a stop, throwing me back like a wrung-out cloth; and with two rasps of engine boost the police cars passed, spurting into the mile-long dip and rise of the Roman road to the coast.

I took my hands from my face and opened my eyes. He had pulled into a lay-by. He switched off. His watch showed quarter past five. The white cuff of his shirt was stained with blood.

He twisted the driving mirror towards me. 'Look at yourself.'

My cheeks and the sides of my nose were covered with thin red smears. I turned up the palms of my hands. The deeper cuts were still bleeding slightly. Trickles had dried down my wrists. There was a rusty smudge at the edge of my skirt, and my ruined stockings stuck to my knees.

Quarter past five. Thirty minutes since I'd run away.

Fifteen miles of twisting lanes, five of Roman road. A last mile at eighty-five with the police closing up behind, impatient, menacing.

The two black cars scorched up the hill in the distance, dwindling, flashing in the sun. I pulled a couple of paper tissues from a box in the pocket, spat on them, and started to wipe my face. He opened the low armrest that divided our seats and brought out a first-aid box which in the sort of accident he seemed to be heading for would have been about as much use as a dolls' hospital.

'It's a gesture,' he said, seeing my look.

I rubbed my knees. The blood slipped off the stockings; it wasn't so easy to clean the skin beneath.

He broke open a roll of gauze. 'Come on, I'll do your hands.'

He leaned across me and unfastened my safety belt. His shirt was sticking to his shoulder blades. I could see the deep regular creases where it had lain folded for so long, formal and forgotten.

He sat back and began to bunch the narrow bandage into a pad. 'You're not going to like this,' he said, tipping up the iodine bottle. 'Hold out.'

The iodine bit the cuts. He stopped for a moment, gripping my wrist. I turned away, in case I should flinch again.

From the lay-by there was nothing to be seen of the estuary; only, overhead, a wide marine sky embossed with pearly clouds, and the slow plumes of the cement works' chimneys; through the windscreen, concrete posts and barbed wire half swamped by chalk-dusted thickets; and behind the fence, breaking the surface of the grey undulations like a bathers' warning, a red rust-pitted disc: POLICE ADVICE—DANGER, KEEP OUT.

'I'll cover the worst cuts,' he said. 'There won't be enough for all of them.'

He opened a tin of adhesive dressings; only the big ones were left. It seemed pointless to put them on so near the end of the journey.

'You'd better have an anti-tetanus injection,' he said, interpreting my hesitation. 'We'll go into Shayle.'

When he'd stuck down the last of the strips he lit a cigarette, the way he did when driving, resting his wrists on the rim of the wheel. He looked at the dried blood on his cuff and moved his hand. There was a smear on the wheel. He rubbed it with the end of the yellow-stained bandage. 'A little blood goes a long way,' he said.

I got out of the car, swinging my feet round puddles in which chalk lay like a sediment; some were filmed with rainbow oil that had seeped from a resting lorry. At the end of the lay-by the thickets behind the barbed wire thinned to a curtain of creeper, then stopped, where the chalk was clawed to within yards of the trunk road. A hundred feet below was the roof of the cement works; one of the cement works, for there were many. The rain had pasted its dust to khaki mud, which in patches was dried by the sun. Beyond the works lay the marsh, and in the middle distance the river, a flat aluminium sheet: the brightest sky could never make it blue.

He came to stand beside me, blowing cigarette smoke at the sulphur rolls that streamed from the chimneys: their eroded lime-caked heads seemed to lean against the sky, toppling backwards. Above the fields behind us a lark unreeled his wiry song. In the stillness after our speed my fear caught up with me, and to stave it off I spoke at random.

'Why did you come?'

He leaned against one of the concrete posts, a common fencing throughout the estuary, giving the place the air of a prison camp.

'I wanted to die.'

I remembered too late the injunction: *don't ask him any questions.* And things were bad enough without my having to think of him dying. I turned away. An Avon tanker came over the hill; the brilliant orange colour makes them visible for miles.

'Not a literal death,' he went on. 'I've sometimes thought of that. But I meant—you know, the fresh start. Ring out the old, ring in the new. It's impossible, it never happened. But you delude yourself that it may. It's a human failing.' He paused. 'I tried. I really tried. Now look at me.'

The tanker roared by. Perhaps if I stopped running and turned to face my fear it would shrink away, as in the old moral fable.

'Then why did you come out? Here, this afternoon?'

He didn't answer. He was holding the cigarette in front of his mouth, staring down into the space beyond the fence. I looked to see what he could see.

The two police cars were passing through the cement works. Perhaps there had been an accident to raise the curve of the monthly graph; someone trapped in machinery or a fall of the quarry face, injured by a misfire of blasting. Nothing seemed amiss. Men, lorries, and grabs moved on the scoured paths as if oiled, their sounds and hesitations smoothed by distance. The police cars were going on, beside the single railway track. An engine puffed to the jetty, dragging four trucks loaded with sacks of cement. If someone had been struck on the line the train would have stopped. Alongside the track was the cable of flying buckets for shipping in bulk, slung across the works over thick rope hammocks, but swinging naked above the marsh, a long double chain almost lost to sight. They hung motionless. The police cars were passing them.

'You,' he said suddenly. 'What brought you out? Curiosity, wasn't it? You wanted to find the truth. And when you found it you didn't like it. You wished you'd spared yourself. Truth! Truth is iodine.'

The police cars had reached the edge of the chalk-pit. Perhaps someone had fallen or jumped from its cliff; or a corpse was floating in one of the disused water-filled pits that lay like bruises on the landscape.

They crawled out on the marsh, slowed by the roughness of the track. Boys might have dared to climb the new pylon, fling stones into the cables, imperilling the grid. Or one of the fires which smouldered on the tips had started to rage out of hand. There might be a breach in the flood wall. Simplest of all, someone had jumped in the river. The estuary was a vast potential menace of danger and sudden death. Police Advice—Danger, Keep Out.

The police cars had stopped. Tiny black men were spreading at the side of the track, a flux of bodies in the glue-like medium of distance; shifting, closing, clustering, wasps in a jam jar.

There was nothing for them to see, nothing but the marsh; a flat wash veined with creeks and ditches feeding and draining the tips, the wastes, the sewers, the mud on which gulls were scattered like crusts for the birds.

I couldn't bear it any longer. 'What do you think they're looking for?' I said. I had to steady my voice. 'Perhaps they're after the Avon wages.'

He gave me an odd look. 'Well, you can be sure *they*

haven't gone out to study the Garganey duck.' He ground his cigarette stub on the concrete post. 'Come on. Let's get your injection.'

The sun had warmed the seats of the open car. My bicycle hadn't shifted on the boot. He pushed at the handlebars, which rested over the occasional seat; they were quite secure.

'I'll take it back before we go to Shayle,' he said.

'Besides I want some things from Woodey's before they close.'

Life must go on.

A lorry raced back to the paper mills, bouncing on its eight wheels, the platform empty except for a pile of tarpaulins neatly strapped behind the cabin. Another was coming up the rise on the outward journey, slow, trembling, distorted by its bulky load of drums.

We drove out of the lay-by, heading for Gunfleet. Gunfleet; below the last contour line, lapped by the river, sequestered in trees, half a mile from the road, cut off from the fringes of Shayle and Culham by two huge horns of the alluvial flats; a decaying village, a single street stricken since Trafalgar, an air lock in time: Gunfleet, where I lived.

I supposed he had some reason for passing the first turning to the village. We went down the drive, past Sankton's garage, which still appeared to be closed, over the chalk-pit bridge.

It was very quiet. Usually there were children dodging among the bushes. The hole was deserted. The swing rope dangled from the bough, its frayed end swinging gently in the breeze. It was cold in the shade. Here the sun hadn't dried out the rain at all.

At the turn of the road I saw Carole running up the slope.

Her sandals were flapping, her skirt was thrust askew by her bony hips. She was not wearing her glasses, and we were almost on her before she recognized us and waved us to stop.

'Have you seen the kids?' she said before we could speak. 'Are they up at the hole?'

'No, it's empty, there's no one about.'

'My God, I'll tan their hides when I find them,' she said, more than usually distraught. She blinked at us and swallowed. 'They've found a girl on the marsh.'

I stared at her lank coppery hair. The wire netting fence behind it was festooned with white bindweed.

'A girl?'

'In a ditch, revolting, dead, stripped, and dumped. Horrible. And the kids are out and I don't know where they are,' she concluded desperately.

Hedley was sitting absolutely still, confounded I suppose, before this flagrantly male outrage.

'But is there any danger?' I said. 'If it's been there some time—and anyway whoever hid it would want to get away—'

'No, no, you don't understand,' she cried. 'It's Lenny. He found it, called his mother, and she ran for the police and now they can't find Lenny. And the children—

'Lenny? You can't think Lenny had anything to do with this? He's harmless, you know he is, everyone knows.'

'But *how* do they know, how could they tell?'

'He wouldn't have led them to it.'

'But they *do,* these odd ones. Don't you remember that case in a park? Can you expect someone like Lenny to act rationally? And if he did only find it, why's he gone off?'

'It's upset him, he's frightened.'

'But that's just as bad. You don't know what it might put in his head. And the children are bound to speak to him if they see him.'

A girl. A girl on the marsh. That was what the police were doing.

'I'll come with you,' I said.

'I'd rather you looked in the village and round the path. If you meet them would you take them home with you till I call?'

'But wandering about alone—'

'I'll be all right. There's more chance of finding them if we both look.'

'I'll come,' Hedley said, stirring himself at last.

'It's no good driving along the road,' Carole said quickly. 'I want to go in the woods.'

'I'll leave the car here.'

'No, you two split up,' she said, starting away. 'One the village, one the path.'

'Don't worry,' I said lamely. 'I'm sure he's harmless.'

'Can't be sure of anything,' she shouted over her shoulder, and ran up the road, a throwback to the stone age, a cave-woman, driven by instinct, almost an animal.

I turned to Hedley. He was leaning forward, resting his arms on the wheel.

'What's the matter?' I said.

He looked at me coldly and drove on without answering. He thought me callous. Perhaps I was. A girl on the marsh. Some unfortunate led on, possibly raped, violated, strangled, and finally crammed in a ditch. It was sickening: I could acknowledge that but not feel it, swamped in my own demoralized collapse, beyond which nothing touched me. The girl on the marsh was a gratuitous twist of circumstance yet appropriate; an example, a symptom, even in my fancy a contagion of erupting trouble: as if the whole of Gunfleet were crumbling at once, caving into darkness and chaos.

We turned the corner by The Ship into the street. They were all out on the pavement, it seemed, by the front doors, appearing strange and half-focused in the afternoon light: it should have been the dusk of evening for them to be standing there, women in pinafores and old men in shirtsleeves. Besides, they were in groups, murmuring, nodding, their eyes furtively seeking the end of the street.

He stopped outside Woodey's. 'I'll take the bike to the cottage and wait for you there.'

'Aren't you going to look for the kids?'

'We'll scout round the path on our way out. You must have the jab.'

I got out of the car. 'That can wait a bit.'

'I'll be at the cottage,' he said.

I walked into the shop. By the shelves half a dozen women stood in a huddle. I knew them all by sight. They were listening to Sally from the railway siding.

'It must be,' she said, 'there's no one apart from him, only ordinary decent people. It's too vile, you'd have seen signs, you'd have seen it coming.'

By *it* she meant the girl on the marsh; the *him* would be Lenny, the odd one, the only suspect Gunfleet could offer. Lenny. Why did it have to be Lenny that found her? But he was always finding things; it was all he could do. I picked a few frozen packets out of the box. Eating goes on through disillusion, misery, and death. Behind me the women clucked like hens: no, there was nothing amiss at all, nowhere tamer than Gunfleet, everyone knew everyone else: there was nothing.

I belonged to Gunfleet, I and mine. Yet they didn't know us, hadn't seen what lay under their very eyes, hadn't sensed the approach in our outwardly quiet lives of what I'd learnt that afternoon; knowledge that knocked the pins out of my existence. They didn't know because there *were* no glaring signs and portents, only domestic curiosities so trivial that even I might have said: there was nothing. So soon, when the police had put a name to the wretched corpse on the marsh, in Shayle or Culham or wherever she came from someone else would protest: there was nothing: no hint of violence, of crime, only the tedious, endless, sordid round of life. There was nothing.

Nothing will come of nothing. That was what Lear said, the old blind, imperious, obstinate king, to the daughter that loved him in silence. Nothing will come of nothing.

I passed on to biscuits. The hens huddled closer, heads nodding up and down, blind and deaf to anything but their horror.

'Did you see her?'

'On the way back.'

'What did she say?'

'Awful, blurting it all out. She couldn't stop.'

I hesitated between shortbread and digestive. The voices sank to whispers.

'And there was blood, after being in the ditch, even. All down.'

'Well if she was struck–'

'It wasn't that.'

'What?'

'Well—you know.'

'Really?'

'I suppose you can be killed any day.'

'If it was rape and she'd never—'

'She said there was a lot. All down. You'd never get that with the ditch.'

'Must have been the usual, then, poor thing.'

I left the shelf, sunk in my own troubles. I put what I'd bought on the counter. It wasn't till then that the meaning of what I'd heard struck me; and in the next second a thought exploded in my mind. I tried to stifle it. Too late. I was engulfed in shapeless billowing fear. I'd put a match to petrol, made a link; appalling, impossible. Possible.

I took my change, nodded to Mrs Woodey, went into the street. It was incredible: no one looked at me, nothing had changed. With distant relief I saw Carole turn the corner, the children running and staggering round her legs.

My heart was beating heavily, not fast. I took a few steps forward, then stopped. I couldn't go to the cottage. I had to think.

I turned towards the river. Out on the flood wall I could sit in peace, alone. The Shayle side of the marsh would be empty as usual.

But I was afraid to go on the marsh, even the Shayle side; especially the lonely Shayle side. I was afraid in spite of myself, afraid of meeting Lenny unhinged by his discovery, Lenny about whom no one could be sure.

Where could I go?

Carole would have given me tea, whisky, as much as I asked; but among the swarming children I could never think, nor could I stop my ears to her ceaseless scatty drawl. Besides, Tubby might come in.

Ian's—Ian's was impossible. How could I go there ever again?

The seats on the Promenade were too close to the street.

Anyone could see me, could come and sit next to me, anyone. I could have taken a bus into Shayle or Culham; but where then? The Ship was closed.

I was tired. I had to sit down alone and think.

There was one place, the last place where they would look for me, one place, ugly, murky, and bare; sanctuary. I crossed the road and slipped in the side door of the church.

There was no one inside, not a soul, no one to see that I failed to perform the rites of which so much is heard. I would have done it if I'd known how; an entrance fee, conscience money for use of a place to which I had no right. I walked beside the rows of benches, out of sight of the door, right to the front, by the altar with its dingy brass vases and crucifix and small curtained cupboard. I dropped my packets on the end of the first seat, slid to my knees on the gritty plank, and put my head in my hands. I wasn't praying. I knew no prayers but the blank formalities of childhood. I was at rest, inviolable. If someone should come in they would leave me alone. I was kneeling as if in penance; that was what I deserved, punishment for my summer of arrogance and vanity. Through crossed fingers I stared at a rack for candles. There were none burning, only a few guttered stubs thick with dust. Half way down the stand was a metal money box, its slot bright at the edges where coins had worn away the paint.

I had to think, examine the summer, sift the past for fragments of memory, sharp, coloured, dimensional, like cubes of mosaic, which separately seemed insignificant; put together they took on meaning, formed a picture itself demanding to be explained, like a dream; or rather a nightmare so dreadful I couldn't bear to explain it. That was weakness, evasion; it had to be faced.

They could be tied together after all, my own troubles and the girl on the marsh, one horror, worse than anything I'd ever known, the worse that could be. It was possible; I had to think whether it were true.

I had to go back to the beginning; though there is never a beginning, only a point when you wake up.

Chapter Two

ONE SATURDAY EVENING WE WERE IN THE SHIP, which seemed no different from what it usually was on Saturday evenings; the public bar crowded with louts from Shayle and Culham; the anachronistic jukebox throbbing softly, a throaty meretricious pulse; smoke seeping through the screen of bottles that divided the two bars. On our side, as usual, we were the only customers.

It must have been the Saturday of the flower show at Shayle. Fellowes the landlord had brought in his prize-winning rose: he wanted Ian to take a photograph. It stood on the counter in a narrow glass with the first-class label still tied round its neck, a single orange bloom, tapered, flawless, living perfection. I remember Ian staring at it. He might have been judging light value, wondering what exposure to give; except that every so often he would brush the outcurved petals with his fingers, so that I knew he was staring because he was overwhelmed with its beauty. He was trying to suck it into his memory. The camera helps; it keeps back something, images, dreams, unsatisfactory as they are, but still something.

I watched his fingers stroke the side of the rose; they had the clean unscarred skin of the office worker. I looked at my own hands. Allowing for the difference of age and sex they were not unlike.

'Not bad,' Hedley said in my ear. 'What annual tonnage of hand cream is consumed in Gunfleet?'

'I only wash up once a day.'

That was my way of dealing with him; answer quickly, preferably flippantly; regret it later.

I took my drink to a wooden settle. The red wallpaper above it gave an illusion of warmth, comfort, and home. On the table lay the solitaire board. It belonged to the pub, an old thing, its wooden frame darkened with decades of fingering, the sockets filled with glass marbles. Only the silvered ball in the centre might have been part of the original equipment. I could never isolate it, no matter how many games I gave myself; if games they could be called. Hedley had played with it when he first came to Gunfleet, sitting in the corner on his own, retiring and shy, as I thought. Now he was nearly always with the others.

The others. They were at the bar, three backsides in grass-stained trousers, each draped with the insignia of its owner, binoculars, camera, vasculum. Tubby, Ian, Tom, in descending order of magnitude; three men, three boys, rigged out in old clothes that they couldn't damage in their play, united in singleminded zeal over their specimens and records and photographs, the collection of which had become a mania, like engine spotting. Even Ian had abandoned the rose to pore over some tattered rag of a plant. The three heads bent together, the bald, the fair, and the black. Tubby, Ian, Tom.

I looked at Hedley; the stranger, the grey head, the solitaire in an old navy-blue shirt and the trousers that seemed always about to slip down. He was watching the others with amusement, innocent not malicious, or so his eyes made it appear; they were so wide set, so pure a blue. I couldn't imagine them concealing anything, couldn't imagine a stain on the mind behind. What he must have been able to get away with in his life, thanks to the chance of having eyes like that!

I began to move the marbles of the solitaire board.

Later he came across to me.

'Any luck?'

'No. Did you ever do it?'

He shook his head. 'I think it's impossible. Would you like another drink?'

'Thank you. The same.'

He leaned across the table, looking at the sepia photograph on the wall. Only from the faded writing on the mount could anyone have known that the four central blobs were seals in the river off Gunfleet, 1911.

'They must have made a navigational error,' I said. 'They're intelligent creatures, they wouldn't come here from choice.'

'Didn't you?'

He had a way of asking apparently idle questions that turned out to be personally loaded. I didn't answer, but followed him to the bar.

He glanced at the large rent in the seat of Tubby's trousers. They had been good trousers once, showerproof, zipped from ankle to calf; below the straining waist-band on either side were strips of slotted elastic in which were stuck a few golf tees. I couldn't believe that Tubby would appear so disreputable in public.

'Do you wear those trousers at Culham Park, Tubby?' I said.

'My dear girl, certainly not.' He looked up from the blade of grass he'd been scrutinizing. 'Why should you think such a thing?'

I picked one of the tees from its slot and held it out.

'Where the devil did that come from?' he said, groping round his waist, or rather his middle.

Hedley smiled. 'How long since you went round?'

'He plays every Friday with Ian,' I said.

Ian looked up. 'What's that?'

'I was saying that you go to Culham Park with Tubby every Friday.'

'Oh. Yes.' He flushed slightly, as if detecting censure. 'It's usually a slack day, I manage to clear everything by lunch. But that reminds me, Tub, I shan't be able to come this week. We're still catching up on the budget.'

He looked flustered. I thought it must be because he expected some sarcasm to follow, and he hated to be ribbed about his work. Someone has to collect customs duty. But he might have spared his anxiety. Hedley wanted to know nothing more than the exact proportion of tax in the price of a gallon of Avon Triple.

'I didn't know you were a motorist,' Ian said.

'I've hardly used the car since I've been here. I keep it up at Sankton's.'

'Then I hope you *do* keep it.' Tubby barely lowered his voice. 'Have you checked the lead in the battery? Chained all movable parts?'

'Now, Tubby,' said Ian, 'nothing's ever been proved against young Sankton.'

They were schoolboys. Ian was the captain, stern but

just, the tall straight-shouldered Englishman whom sentimentalists like to think typical, but who is so rare.

I looked at him. He was thirty-eight. His hair had only slightly thinned in the six years that I'd known him; it was still the same pale yellow colour, as if it had been bleached. But the lines on his face had deepened, especially round his mouth. He still smiled, of course, with all his moving, disturbing charm; disturbing not in itself, but in its strength, and in the unexpectedness of its coming from Ian. I couldn't acquit him of being conscious of it; but he did curb what most men cultivate once some luckless female has let them know they possess it.

'Agnes, how's your driving going on?' said Tubby. 'I haven't heard any grinding crashes lately. Has she passed the stage of initial disorder, Tom?'

My husband looked up from the newspaper on which were spread the plants they'd collected. He'd been embellishing a face in one of the advertisements with glasses and a moustache. A schoolboy. A fourth-former.

'She's not too bad,' he said, 'needs practice, that's all.'

'I can't practise alone,' I said, 'it's against the law.'

Tubby seized his glass and stared at me dramatically. 'Agnes! Am I coming between you? I feel it—he's neglecting you to collect my soil samples.'

'I'm used to it,' I said. If there hadn't been soil samples there would have been something to take Tom out on the marsh all the long evenings of summer; studying, measuring, comparing from one year, one month, almost one day to the next, the minute changes in its fauna, flora and ecology.

'My name's down for the test,' I said in private despair.

Tom picked up his pencil and returned to marginal scribbles.

'You can't expect to pass first shot. Hardly anyone does.'

'Why don't you go to a driving-school?' Ian said.

Tubby laughed. 'Agnes is afraid of swearing in front of an instructor.'

'I'm short of money.' It was no more than the truth.

'What do you want with soil samples?' Hedley asked Tubby.

'You haven't seen our experiment, you must, all laid out in my attic. You take the highest level of the salt marsh, the part that only gets submerged at the equinox, and at the solstice—'

'The point furthest in time from the equinox,' Tom explained.

'Get away!' said Hedley, with ironical wonder.

I felt myself turn scarlet.

'At the solstice,' Tubby resumed patiently, 'you take samples of soil from that level and test the salinity of soil water to see what extent it's been altered. If there's been a lot of rain naturally the salt solution has been diluted, after long drought the concentration is high.'

'Do you need experiments to work that out?'

'Ah, but the osmotic pressure of halophytes, salt marsh plants, changes in response to the surrounding medium. They're adapted for survival. So you see—'

Tubby was carried away by enthusiasm, far above my head. A schoolboy, with a science kit; the fat loafer with the disconcerting brain.

He stopped short, in the middle of a sentence as far as I could tell, suddenly deflated.

'Of course what we do is only the crudest simplest amateur stuff. Childish almost. Do you know some of the choicest brains in the country are working on halophytes?' His eyes were quite wistful. 'Osmosis, that's their line. Everyone knows what it is. But *how*? How exactly does it happen?'

This biochemical poser which was engaging some of the choicest brains in the country was addressed to Hedley. He did not seem sorry to hear Fellowes calling time.

We parted as usual, Hedley going through the door at the back of the private bar, for he was staying at The Ship; the rest of us into the street, as the louts disgorged with harmless noise into the soft evening, still luminous with sunset, but shadowed by night coming up the river.

Chapter Three

THERE WAS AN AFTERNOON WHEN I WENT UP TO Sankton's garage; it couldn't have been long after, perhaps even the next day, for it was a Sunday. As he was going out to the marsh Tom had asked me to get some polish for the car; and although by going on Sunday I knew I should be safe from seeing Sankton I changed into a dress with long sleeves and a high collar. I used to wear it for supervising examinations, before I gave up teaching.

I must have taken the path from our cottage through the old chalk-pit because I remembered stepping through the gap between two of the lock-up sheds in which Sankton keeps his second-hand cars and general rubbish, coming out on the cinder patch behind the main building.

A car stood in front of the open door of one of the sheds, a white two-seater gleaming in the sun. The bonnet was raised, and bending over the engine with his back to me was Hedley. He looked round as my feet crunched on the cinders, and stood up.

'Hullo,' he said. 'Tubby alarmed me with his talk of pilfered lead.'

'Everything in order?'

'So far.'

I remembered the old dress I was wearing, and that I'd wiped off my lipstick. I wished I'd gone round by the road.

'I like your car,' I said. 'How can you bear to let it lie here idle?'

'It makes a change for me not to be in it.' He wiped a bird dropping from the paint. 'Absence makes the heart grow fonder.'

'Out of sight, out of mind,' I countered; though if ever a proverb lied, that one does.

He leaned against the side of the car, half sitting on the door, and rubbed his arm across his forehead. He hadn't had his hair cut since he came, and with his bending over the engine, it had fallen forward, lank strips of it, the colour of aluminium. Only two buttons were left on his khaki shirt, so bleached and frayed, it might have seen service in the desert.

'Would you teach me to drive?' I asked.

'In this?' He looked outraged.

'No, I meant in my own car, sit with me while I practise. I can drive already.' I was overcome with horror at what I'd done, but it was too late, I had to go on. 'You heard Tom say he hasn't time.'

'And you think I've nothing to do with my evenings.'

I wasn't going to deny this; for he did have nothing to do, as far as anyone could see. He was teaching himself Russian, we all knew that; but no one can cram Russian for sixteen hours a day. Besides, I'd often seen him idling about the beach by Ancrum's yard.

'It wouldn't have to be evening,' I said. 'Any time when you were free.'

'You'll ask Tom to go to work on the bus, then?'

'I've got a car of my own.' I was amazed no one had regaled him with that particular village scandal; but they'd seen the car so little that perhaps they were beginning to forget it was there in our garage, next to the Mini-Minor that went with Tom's job at the Shayle Museum.

'Yet you're too hard up to have lessons?' he said.

'That's why. I blew nearly everything on the car.'

'I wouldn't do it without dual control, however well you think you can drive.'

'All right,' I said, 'it doesn't matter. I'm sorry.'

'What for?'

'Bothering you.'

'You're the one that's bothered.'

It was true; and how I detested him for saying it. I walked across the yard. The cinder dust worked between my sandal straps, my collar and sleeves clung to me. I could hardly remember, when I reached the forecourt of the garage, what I'd come for.

Cars and motor bikes were still belting along the main road, their owners intent on an hour by the torpid sea. There was only one car at the pumps. The driver had got out to look at the radiator; only seeing Livia he'd stopped in his tracks.

She was squatting by one of the tubs that held geraniums, painting it yellow. Her dungarees were splashed with paint. Her hair was swept off her forehead into a small dome, and hung like satin ribbons between her shoulders where the straps crossed. The white sleeves of her tee shirt barely capped her arms.

Stand up, Livia, I thought, turn round, devastate him. I'd seen so many drivers pull in, grinning, ready to whistle and quip or try for some cruder familiarity, seen their mouths freeze and their faces go blank as something took them by the throat and squeezed hard. Well, something—there was no need to be vague. Yet it wasn't entirely the superlative of lust. She was simply a living perfection, flawless, graceful, and warm. It seemed to me that the grossest, most inarticulate clod couldn't be immune to her beauty.

As if she'd heard my thoughts she did stand up, carried the pot of paint round to the back of the sheds. On an impulse I followed her. I wanted to see Hedley's reaction.

She'd gone to fetch another can and some rag. He crossed the yard towards her. He had his back to me, but I saw that he must have spoken, because she stood listening like a polite child, looking at the ground, her eyebrows making a line at right angles with her little hawk nose. She shook her head, and with a word or two and the brief smile she gave customers when the pumps were busy she walked away.

A door opened in the long shed beyond Hedley. A man appeared, a remarkable man; like an animal, I thought at once, and had no time for more because with a look at all of us that was intense, concentrated in a way I couldn't analyse, he stepped back and slammed the door of the shed behind him. Hedley hadn't moved. Something in the set of his shoulders reminded me inexplicably of the mortifying episode of my driving proposals. Livia was coming back. She hadn't seen me, and without knowing why, I didn't want her to. I darted back to the forecourt.

I bought the polish for Tom. I also asked whether they could fit dual control to my car, how long it would take, how much it would cost; and having satisfied myself that it was possible on all counts, I went back by the drive. It was the Gothick approach to Gunfleet, spanning by a bridge the tangled chasm of the old chalk-pit, winding between crags of chalk and woods thick with ivy, skirting the hole, that bare-sided hollow littered with milk crates and old tyres, where children swung dangerously from side to side on a rope fastened to an overhanging bough. It was the long way round to the cottage, taking me half through the village.

At the turn of the road I met Ian. I was surprised that he wasn't out on the marsh. He was carrying a half-gallon can; its top was furred with dust and fluff.

'Are you going to throw that in the hole?' I said.

He looked confused, and brushed the can against the grass verge. 'As a matter of fact I'm taking it to Sankton's for some paraffin.'

The sun was blazing above us, as it had done for weeks.

'What on earth for?'

'Oh, cleaning,' he said vaguely.

'Go round by the back, you'll see a pretty sight, Hedley with his car. Hedley's car.' I corrected myself, but not before he'd shot me a quick look.

'What make?' he asked.

'Couldn't tell you. White, fast, with a hood. I know nothing about cars. In any respect.'

He smiled. His grey eyes were almost unbearable to me in their expression of affection.

'It's quite simple,' he said. 'All you need to remember is that you have two feet, neither heavier than the other.'

If only that were all! He would have liked a car, I knew that. And I understand the little vanity, the face-saving pride that made him keep his driving licence, though he had long since had to part with his father's pre-war car with the sphinx on the bonnet. I wanted to say: take mine. I'll give it to you. But of course I couldn't.

'Hullo, here's Lenny,' he said, looking over my shoulder, 'and I think he has a *trouvaille*.'

The enormous figure was coming down the slope at its invariable jogtrot. His fat chin was shaking, glistening with sweat. He wore a red tartan shirt that was far too small for him, stretched tight under his armpits. His mother dressed him in what she could lay hands on, oddments from church jumble sales. It struck me that in hot weather he couldn't know what it was to feel comfortable.

'Hullo, Lenny,' Ian said.

Lenny stopped. His smile was permanent, but it widened. 'Good afternoon.' That was what we knew he'd said; no stranger could have interpreted the gobbled sounds.

'What's that you've got?' Ian went on.

The grin stretched even wider. The bright watery eyes wavered in bliss. He unclosed his fist. In his palm lay a small split flint with a patch of white crystals in the centre of each half.

'That's very nice, Lenny,' said Ian. 'Where did you find it?'

I knew it was an effort for him to be patient with the great shambling creature. He hadn't Tom's determined gentleness, nor the scientific curiosity of Tubby. But he would never pass Lenny on the other side. Oh captain, my captain!

The poor idiot concluded a long mumbling rigmarole, impossible to understand, and held out the flint.

'Malcolm,' he said distinctly.

'Oh, I see. Thank you.' Ian took it with well-simulated gratitude. 'I'll give it to him when I get in. He'll be very pleased.'

'Good-bye,' Lenny gobbled, and set off down the road at his loose heavy run.

'I'll have to get rid of it,' Ian said. 'He's always giving me stones for Malcolm, the house is littered with them.'

My poor love, you've been told not to bring them in, haven't you? I thought.

'Throw it in the trees.'

'No, he might recognize it. You can't hurt the poor chap's feelings.'

'Wait till you're on the marsh then drop it in the river,' I suggested.

'Yes, that's best. I must get up and view this scintillating car. See you later, Ag.'

Ag. Loathsome abbreviation, intolerable from anyone but Ian. Didn't he notice that only he was allowed to use it? I wanted to tell him. Couldn't anyone understand why I wanted to tell him?

I turned into the path behind his house. In the garden Malcolm was shouting: 'Dad! Dad!'

'He's up the road,' I called. 'What do you want?'

Malcolm skipped from the outhouse where Ian has his darkroom. 'Oh hullo.' He stuck his head round the kitchen door. 'Mum, Agnes says he's up the road. Shall I go and fetch him?'

Helen must have said yes, because he ran across the lawn towards me. 'Whereabouts?'

'He'll be up at the hole by now. What's the matter?'

'He's wanted on the phone.'

Helen came into the garden. She was wearing one of her uniforms, I forget which, she seems to have so many.

'Hullo, I thought Ian was in the shed. Where was he going?'

'I don't know. Just walking.'

She frowned. 'Well, shall I tell them to hold on? How far up was he?'

'Not far. Malcolm will catch him.'

She went into the house.

I walked back to the road and waited. After a minute Malcolm came racing round the bend with Ian. He must have put down the paraffin can, for he didn't have it with him.

I went down to The Ship. Lenny was sitting on the flint wall by the bus stop, waiting to see the bus from Shayle to Culham, which at every other hour makes the detour to Gunfleet. A tug hooted on the river, nasally, like a donkey that had forgotten the first half of his cry. No one was about. The village basked in the silence of Sunday afternoon between two and seven. I opened my handbag. By a stroke of luck there was a toffee loose at the bottom. No one would see me.

'Lenny,' I said handing it to him quickly, 'here, take it.'

He stood up, towering above me. His bald red head glistened in the sun, his scurfy face was wreathed in the unending smile.

'Thank you very much,' he gobbled.

Fumbling at the wrapping with his clumsy paws he lolloped away to the Promenade. That was where I had first seen him, six years before. I was walking alone, right out on the flood wall, when he scrambled up from the marsh, face to face with me, gigantic, shambling, grinning. I'd never been so frightened in my life. Poor Lenny. I thought my hour had come.

Was it that Sunday, or another, when I sat on the Promenade correcting papers? The same, I think, later in the afternoon.

I sat on the second seat from the village, opposite a row of small shoes on the edge of the river wall; their owners paddled out of sight, picking over the drift-wood, bottles, and oily stones that compose what's known as the beach, occasionally coming up to take a turn on the swings. Without raising my eyes I could tell when this happened, from the rhythmic mouth-organ squeal of the iron bars.

I put the last paper on the pile, stretched, and glanced along the Promenade. Hedley was sitting on the next seat.

'Have you finished?' he said.

'Yes. Did you want this bench?'

He often sat there; perhaps that was why I'd chosen it.

He came across to me. 'I didn't want to disturb you, that's all.' He looked at the papers. 'I didn't know you were a teacher.'

'I'm not, now. These are correspondence courses, and the worst of my batch. Absolute nits, and *King Lear* as set text.'

'Absolute nits,' he repeated.

I don't know what drove me to be stupid when I was with him, show myself up in the vilest light, even to say things I didn't really mean.

'Why didn't you stay a teacher?' he went on. 'Too lazy?'

There was no need to be ashamed of myself, he was almost as bad.

'The museum doesn't like working wives.'

I could rarely stop myself answering his questions, no doubt because he took it so much for granted that I should. He had the power of compelling admissions; perhaps he was an inquisitor, a retired or resting brain-washer.

'You're still working,' he said.

'Not going out. The appearance is what counts. Anyway it's not full time, not what I call working. I don't earn much.'

'Enough to give you a sense of independence.'

I settled the papers in my arm.

'Don't let me keep you from getting Tom's supper,' he said.

I hated his irony. 'He's on the marsh. He won't be in yet. There's a patch on Culham Long Level completely unspoilt, natural salt marsh. They watch over it like a baby.'

'You're not interested?'

I shrugged. 'I'd rather have the cement works. It's ugly, but at least there are people. The marsh is ugly and empty.'

'Get away. It's full of plants and birds.'

'Nature! the most overrated melancholy thing. On and on, the same old cycle, year in year out, senseless, changeless, unreasoning growth and decay. They toil not, neither do they spin, that's what I have against the creatures of nature. Oh, I know, they build nests and perform prodigies of adaptation and survival. But it's all for themselves, to reproduce themselves. How can you respect them for that?'

'And what do humans produce that you respect?'

'Art.'

'In the cement works?'

'In general.'

He looked out at the marsh. 'I can't say it's positively inviting. I suppose it appeals to the devoted, like Tom, or a scientist like Tubby. But if you were to see some natural beauty pure and unspoilt–'

'Unspoilt? In England?'

'There's still the north-east coast. Though even there now, gets littered with caravans.'

This was too much for me. 'We'll be doing just that in a few weeks,' I said.

'Oh, is it yours, the caravan behind the cottage?' He wasn't in the least abashed. 'Where are you going?'

'I don't know, just setting off. We could go right up and defile this precious pure coast.'

'I wish I hadn't told you.'

'If no one went there, no one would know it was beautiful.'

'You might as well stay away. *You* won't appreciate it. Your vitiated taste will clamour for the works of man. Hotels, beach huts, soft drinks. Promenades.'

I had to smile with him. We looked along Gunfleet's sole amenity. The Promenade. A half-mile strip of parched grass, embellished with ornate Edwardian benches from which the white paint was flaking, cast-offs of some thriving resort, a bargain to assure the poor of Gunfleet that they were not neglected; on a level with the children's two swings and iron maypole from which all but three of the chains were broken. Few people sat here, even in summer. They walked, though, taking the Promenade literally, exercised their dogs along the convenient length of cracked concrete path. I turned to survey the whole of it; and thus I saw Livia come between the iron posts that ended the street.

She seldom came down to the village now, when she was off duty. She'd changed into a sleeveless brown dress. It was impossible to tell whether she wore stockings. All her skin—face, neck, arms, legs—was the same; olive silk. Her figure had perfect balance, she was neither small nor, like me, gangling tall. Her hair, once fair, had darkened to a smoky colour while mine turned slowly to mouse. Why didn't I hate her? For I didn't.

She returned my smile and greeting very quietly, seeming embarrassed. I hesitated whether to speak and she walked on.

I glanced at Hedley. He was looking after her; and the naked wish in those pure blue eyes was so intense that it frightened me. I sat down on the bench, blank with shock, a weak-kneed fool.

'What's the matter?' he said.

'I just caught the blast of that Biblical look you gave Livia.'

To see a man blush so violently was a novelty. I thought I might try to make him do it again.

'I'm sorry,' he said. 'Biblical? Whatever do you mean?'

'Not the parts that get set for G.C.E.'

'I see. When some worthy says *Come lie with me, my sister*.'

It was my turn to blush. I stood up and walked to the edge of the wall, to the broken steps by the break-water.

He followed me. 'Everyone looks at Livia,' he said.

Everyone: but not all quite like that.

'How long has she been here?'

'Nearly two years. Since she left the hospital—no, I forgot, she was a few months on the glove counter at Denning's first.'

'What was wrong? Why was she in hospital?'

'She wasn't a patient, she trained as a nurse for a year.'

'And gave up?'

'She failed some exam. Besides, I think she didn't like the discipline. She hates to be tied. Strange, she's so quiet.'

'Still waters,' he said. 'Where does she come from?'

'She's half Italian. Her father was naturalized, I believe. Must have been, because she would have been born some time in the war, she's twenty-one. Anyway he went back afterwards. They've been separated years, her parents.'

'What I meant to ask was whether she's a local girl.'

'Poor Livia, she has no place. She's moved all over the country following mother, from one potty private school to another picking up shreds of education, then drifting in and out of unsatisfactory jobs. Finally the nursing fiasco.'

'I wonder what made her think she'd like that.'

'Mother. The advantage was that Livia would have somewhere to live so that *she* could go to Canada. Livia's always been rather an encumbrance, I imagine.'

'How did you learn all this?'

'Livia told me. At least, the facts, I've made the inferences. Not unjustly, I think. Her mother's still out there. Livia went to a hostel in Culham when she left the hospital, one of Helen's welfare societies runs it. I don't think she liked it much better than the nurses' home. She moved as soon as she could. I suppose that is why she works at Sankton's. Better pay.'

My voice took on colour in spite of my effort to keep it neutral. He raised his eyebrows: he never missed an inflection.

'Don't you approve?' he said.

'I don't rule her life for her. I expect she can take care of herself. With looks like that she'd have had to learn young.'

The brown figure was superb, even at a distance. 'I've never seen anyone so beautiful as Livia,' I said. 'Sometimes I think she'll dissolve like a mirage. All those molecules trembling in their own chance perfection—it seems impossible it should hold.'

I'd have given almost anything to look like that; I with measurements that sounded all right till they were stretched over five foot nine, with freckles, glasses, and an armful of essay papers.

Carole came out of their garden towards us. Among the dozen filthy bare-legged children on the beach were all four of Tubby's; the boys crawling over the hulks of two barges drawn up on the shingle to rust, the girls playing on the green-stained sluice, round which little waves broke like claws curling and retracting: the waves of a medieval illumination, except for their cough-medicine colour.

'Come on, you kids,' Carole shouted, 'if you want any tea you'll have to come and get it. Bloody brats,' she went on, turning to us, 'I told them not to stay out long. Kimbold Anna's having her litter and I have to come out hunting for them. *Will* you get a move on!' she bawled.

The little girls climbed the broken steps slowly, because their legs were short. Tansy the baby was in front, pushed from behind on the plump wad of a skirt stuffed into knickers. Carole leaned down, showing two inches of embroidered petticoat embossed with grime, and pulled her up the last step, scraping her legs against the wall. Tansy flinched and opened her mouth to cry; then clamped it shut, square, repressing the protest which in three years she'd learnt to be futile. She had a little sore place between the corner of her mouth and her nostril.

Carole strode back to the house, dragging the child beside her. 'Bring the shoes,' she called to Sorrel. 'The boys can do without. You shouldn't have taken them off.'

I looked along the Promenade. Livia had nearly reached the end of the path. It continued as the flood wall for a further mile as far as the jetty of the paper mills. Beyond that, in the distance, cranes, funnels, and the bulk of a liner's hull loomed from the flatness of the docks at Shayle; and beyond that, out of sight on the next reach, lay the Avon refinery, a smudge on the opaline sky.

I wanted to be gone before Livia turned back. Whether he stayed was his affair.

I went down to the street that evening, to see if the men were coming. The sky was the colour of sugared almonds, orange, pink, and mauve. The old women stood with folded arms at the doors; the old men, smoking, hovered round their runner beans; and between the marigolds sat motionless neutered cats. Woodey's wireless sounded from an open window, some soprano launching emotion into the air. At the end of the street a car started. I could hear the dim throb of the jukebox from The Ship.

I walked down there, thinking that they might have gone in for a drink before coming home. Outside motor bikes were clustered like metallic flies. There was even a tangle of pedal bikes against the wall. They always come to us at week-ends, the louts from Shayle and Culham, amuse themselves by poking us in the ribs. It makes a change from the eternal burn-up along the Roman roads. They never come in the week; by then they have less money.

Hedley's car was parked at the corner. He was in the bar, with Ian and Tubby; but not Tom.

'My dear Agnes, you've come in search of your beloved,' Tubby said, the moment I appeared. 'He asked me to tell you he'd be along soon, but I hadn't got round to it, as you see.'

He went on where he'd been interrupted, assuring Ian that beyond possibility of error he had heard a whimbrel.

I asked Fellowes to put my drink on the slate. Beyond a nod when I first came in Hedley had ignored me. He was drinking two to my one, perhaps to drive away the melancholy that seemed to be gouging his face. His arm rested on the counter; sinews, hair, and a steel wrist-watch, the formula of devastation; aimed at, achieved, and forgotten.

Tubby continued to prattle ornithology. Shelduck were

present, three separate pairs of snipe had towered, two pairs of ringed plovers were breeding. I finished my drink, and contemplating a second, looked at Hedley. His face was blank with surprise at something behind me.

I turned. Livia was standing on the threshold as if she wanted to join us but lacked courage. Her eyes seemed extraordinarily large and brilliant. From the other bar the louts began to whistle and call out. She flushed, hesitated for a moment, then walked away.

I wondered if she'd wanted to speak to me. Twice in the day I'd avoided her, twice she'd seen me next to Hedley and perhaps hadn't cared to approach. I went to the door, but I was too late. She'd crossed the road. Helen's van had pulled up beside her and Helen was speaking, perhaps to offer a lift. I turned round quickly, colliding with Hedley. He swerved, tripped on the step at the door, and fell against the bicycles stacked by the wall. The whole pile shuddered, scraped, and shifted; and he picked himself up while Helen and Livia were still turning to stare at the noise.

'Curse,' he said quietly.

'I'm sorry,' I said. 'That was my fault.'

'Don't forget I've been drinking.'

He didn't look drunk. His speech was perfectly clear, slightly clipped as always. I helped him to push the bicycles back.

Helen opened the door of the van. Livia got in, reluctantly, I thought. She was still flushed, she seemed upset. I glanced at Hedley, but he was looking at his hand. There was a neat gash nearly an inch long on the outer cushion of the palm. He must have struck it on some sharp metal part of the machines, possibly a pedal tread.

'I didn't know they had a van,' he said as Helen drove off.

'It belongs to one of her societies, she drives it around Culham two afternoons a week on some welfare business. Today must have been an extraordinary occasion. I suppose she's taking it back. Livia has a room in Culham.'

I stopped short. Why tell him that? Why did I do it?

We went into the bar. 'Tubby, don't you think something ought to be done to this cut?' I said. I turned to Hedley. 'Show him.'

He wiped his hand on his trousers and held it up, humouring me. A thick red tear welled out and ran down his wrist. Ian looked away quickly.

'I say, old man, you're going to need a stitch in that,' said Tubby. 'No no, seriously. Let me see.' He took Hedley's hand and moved the flesh between his fingers, causing the gash to open: to smile, I thought, wondering what it looked like when they drew a scalpel right across the thorax. 'Oh yes, not a doubt,' Tubby concluded cheerfully. 'I'll run you over to Culham.'

He overrode Hedley's protests by sheer volubility. Hedley oughtn't to drive to worsen the cut, the bus was too slow, if he didn't have Tubby to pass him up the line he'd sit for hours in casualty with the other poor bastards, old Benger would be on duty and would do a neat job on any friend of Tubby's because he knew that if he didn't Tubby would take his time when next Benger wanted a report in a hurry from the path lab. Hedley succumbed. We all went to the door.

'Do you want to take my car?' Hedley asked.

'So that's yours,' said Tubby. 'Sex on four wheels. Must go like a dingbat. I'll stick to what I'm used to, thanks. Shan't be a jiffy.'

Ian's face was pale. He was careful not to look at the hand

which Hedley held up in an attempt to slacken the bleeding. We waited in silence. What had been orange in the west had darkened to smoky ochre, though above us it was still light. The river reflected the sky like a glass, its medicine-water transmuted to pallid green which lightened the windows of the Georgian house facing the Promenade; that house of soft brick and warped slate roof which sheltered Tubby and Carole and their brood of children and animals.

The chains of the maypole clanged on the post as some late-playing brat abandoned them. Tubby brought the Jag round the corner, pulled up beside us, and opened the door.

'Wait a minute.' He passed his hand over the passenger seat and threw something into the gutter. 'Kids,' he muttered. 'All right.'

Hedley sat down and shut the door. The window was open on his side.

Tubby was always prompt to strike up conversation, 'I say,' he began, 'do you follow the turf?'

He drove away.

I looked in the gutter at my feet. What he'd thrown out was a half-chewed toffee. It might have been worse; in that car it often was.

Chapter Four

It must have been the next day, a Monday therefore, when I sat marking and reading in the cottage till my evening meal. Yes, it was Monday: I remember eating a cold loin chop held like a sandwich to save washing-up; and afterwards I set out to walk along the Promenade. At the corner by The Ship I saw an odd group coming down the drive: Hedley, Helen, and Marian, a fat child of about twelve from the other end of the street. I waited hoping that Helen might take the back path; but they came on together.

'I've complained to the council before,' Helen was saying. 'They should fence it in. Perhaps now they'll listen. It's too much to hope that the children will learn a lesson.'

The child had been crying, was still sniffing and rubbing her eyes. 'What's the matter?' I said.

'Come along, Marian, I'll take you home,' Helen said briskly. She cast a quick glance over my dress, which she disapproved, and walked off down the street.

'What happened?' I asked Hedley.

'She was swinging over the hole and went on too long,

lost momentum, couldn't get back. I was coming away from Sankton's and a couple of boys came racing up the road. They frightened the life out of me, said she was hanging. I thought they meant by the neck.'

'It would be Marian,' I said. 'She must weigh half a ton, great coarse blowsy thing, just like a side of bacon. I'd have let her drop. She'll be a right trollop in two years.'

'You're not very consistent. Only yesterday mankind was the summit of creation. Anyway, why the two-year delay?' he concluded cynically.

I was annoyed to have appeared naïve. 'How did you get her up?'

'I didn't. Malcolm had run home for Helen. She was out on the bough, hauling in. All I did was slither down to stand underneath in case the girl let go at last.'

I looked up the road after Helen; a stocky figure with bulging calves and thighs and great packs of muscle on hips and shoulders that distorted whatever she wore into shapelessness.

'She's strong,' he observed, following my glance.

'She was a P.E. instructress in the army. She still runs keep-fit classes in Culham, two evenings a week.'

'She leads a busy life.'

'She enjoys it.'

He was fidgeting with the bandage on his hand; after twenty-four hours it was loose and rather grubby. He lifted the edge and looked underneath. 'I think I've set it bleeding.'

'Don't show Ian, blood makes him sick. He can't help it. He was just born that way.'

'I thought he looked green last night.' He paused. 'Shall we have a drink? I feel I deserve one for intending a rescue even if I didn't achieve it.'

We walked towards The Ship.

'Tubby told me that Ian was at Cassino,' he said. 'How did he cope with that lot?'

'He'd make himself put up with it, that's all.'

'Call of duty.'

'Yes, he volunteered,' I said, nettled. 'No doubt you waited till you were conscripted.'

'I didn't have long to wait.'

He gave me one of those looks that I thought he must practise before a glass, quick, sideways, with brows drawn down. 'Fond of your brother-in-law, aren't you? First sparing, then defending.'

Fortunately we were at the door of the bar. We went in, and there were Ian and Tubby. Why couldn't they have been on the marsh?

'Hullo Ag,' said Ian. 'Is Tom out?'

'He's working late. What have you got there, Tubby?'

He was holding a very young kitten, one of Carole's Abyssinians.

'Fennel was so inconsiderate as to drop a chair on its tail when it was a week old,' he said. 'If I don't find someone who doesn't mind taking a cat with a rear question mark I shall have to slip the poor creature a cyanide pill. And that's a potential ten quid down the drain.'

Hedley passed me my drink; he knew by now what I wanted without having to ask. He held out his hand for the kitten and Tubby shoved it along the counter. Its paws splayed on the slippery wood. It went to Hedley very readily, nuzzling its head against his arm, crawling up his shirt. No doubt it liked to be stroked by those nice hands, larger and bonier than Ian's, but just as sensuous.

The week-end was over. Both bars were quiet. There

were only a few seamen on the other side, from the Dutch freighter that had put into Ancrum's yard for repair. Tubby was delivering a monologue on the geography of disease, in particular the areas in which cretinism was prevalent.

Hedley glanced about him.

'What is it?' said Tubby.

'Just making sure Lenny's father isn't in earshot.'

'That isn't cretinism, it isn't even congenital. Lenny went that way after an illness when he was a child. I don't know what, I wasn't here, of course, it was thirty years ago. Meningitis, perhaps, or some encephalitis. Just a little sport on the part of the gods. Not even the sins of the fathers, for once. Mind you there isn't the syph that there was. They clear it up. But you do still see its effects, especially among the older generation—heirs to the days of universal morality.'

Ian flushed. I thought it must be because he considered it an improper subject to be discussed in front of me, poor Ian.

'Anyway, it's only a *qualitative* change,' Tubby went on. 'Cholera, diphtheria, gone. T.B., polio, on the run, making way for the next lot. And we should get them cleared out just in time to deal with mutations. Ah, Tubby, Tubby, no rest for you! Chained to the lab all the days of your life, instead of—'

'Instead of what, then?' I asked.

'My dear Agnes, I really couldn't say,' he said with rather sad humour. 'An endless sojourn on the Farne Islands, perhaps.'

Hedley put down his glass. 'When I was a lad I used to dread being sent to the tripe shop. The couple that owned it had an idiot daughter, she used to stand in the door of the room backing the shop—'

'But what were you sent for?' I asked.

'Tripe.'

'Not to eat?'

'When we were well off.'

'What horrible place was this?'

His eyes glinted at me for a second. 'Back there, among the barbarians.' He moved his head a fraction to the north. 'Where were you born, duchess?'

Tubby's foot jammed down on his, a tactful hint to be silent that I could have seen a mile off. Ian leaned across and kissed me on the cheek.

'In a fortunate hour, in the graces' bower, with beauty and goodness and love as her dower,' he said, and smiled at me with all his sweetness.

'Ian, that doggerel I positively identify as coming from one of last year's Christmas crackers,' said Tubby. 'I suppose that's what you call a *bon-bon mot*. We'll have drinks all round to celebrate your wit and good memory.'

He waved his hand to attract the attention of Fellowes from the other bar; and my mental lockjaw relaxed to the extent of letting me move. I went across to the bench and sat under the photograph of ice floes off Gunfleet, 1903. I wished I could have jumped in to cool myself down. Tubby brought my drink and put it on the table without a word. Ian looked as if he would commiserate. Hedley stroked the kitten.

I'd nearly finished the glass when Tom looked in at the door. I stood up.

'Don't hurry,' he said, 'finish your drink.'

Ian turned round quickly at the sound of his voice. It struck me that he'd been waiting for Tom, that he wanted particularly to see him.

I drained the glass. 'I'll get your supper. Ten minutes?'

He nodded. We'd been married six years. Words were superfluous to most of our daily needs.

After supper he went out again. Ian had something to show him before the last light faded, something that couldn't have waited a day, some alien casual weed sprouting from a rubbish tip on the road to Shayle.

When I'd washed up I went at last for my walk along the Promenade. It was the sort of night that fills me with restlessness to go somewhere, anywhere; when I never know what I want except that it isn't to go indoors to bed, to fall asleep. I walked the half-mile and back, and sat down on the second seat.

Gunfleet was dark. One gas lamp cast a tarnished pool on the posts at the end of the path. But the distant shore was laced with lights, white, green, and orange. A launch moved downstream, bright against the strung beads, sinister in its silent gliding; the sound of its engines was swallowed by space. A minute later the wash slapped and sucked among Ancrum's barges, rocking the boats moored to the buoys, raising a smell of weed, mud, and oil. Even here, filth-polluted, the river had a certain freshness; it ran to the sea, the salt-heaving sea with its boundless freedom.

In the docks at Shayle a liner sounded its deep fruity note. Someone was whistling behind me: Tubby coming home. I whistled back. He stopped, came across and sat down beside me.

'Unattended?' he said. 'I've been talking about you.'

'To whom?'

'The mystery man. Giving him your life history.'

'Enthralling for him.'

'He was overcome to learn exactly how he'd put his foot in it.'

'You shouldn't have told him. What does it matter?'

'I said you'd been deprived of love in your childhood.'

'Oh Tubby, that old guff! I'm ashamed of you.'

'If you'd give me time to finish. You're too apt to underestimate my intelligence, Agnes, I hope you're aware of that.' He paused. 'I meant a two-way deprivation. You *weren't* loved. But also you had nothing and no one to give your love to, your yearning little soul was surrounded by inadequate indifferent idols. And look at the result. Never enough praise and attention, never enough luxuries, never enough conquests and heroes.'

'Sheer greed,' I said, as lightly as I could. 'Did you expound all this to Hedley?'

'He was most sympathetic.'

Across the river small red coronets hung in the black sky; warning lights on the giant pylons and power-house chimneys. 'Can you make him out, Tubby?'

'My dear, I can no more place that man than I could shin up yonder mast. I thought you'd know about him. You or Tom.'

'Tom's in the dark. Just happened out of the blue on one of his days at the refinery. Walter asked to see the report, and when Tom arrived in the office there was this fellow, obviously a friend of Walter, who introduced him. They talked about Gunfleet, Hedley said it sounded the ideal place for him to retire to learn Russian undisturbed, and was there anywhere to stay—and well, there he is at The Ship. Till the engineers come, anyway.'

'I think he's a spy.'

'That's the vulgar opinion, I'm surprised you admit to sharing it. On account of the Russian?'

'More that he's a friend of Walter's. After all, Avon security is tantamount to national security.'

'He doesn't look like the friend of a refinery manager. Lacking affluence.'

'Auld lang syne, perhaps. Besides, he must have money to be able to loaf about all these weeks, lucky beggar, even if he doesn't put it on his back. Can't we quiz him, see what we can unearth?'

'Walter said not to ask him any questions.'

'Aha!' Tubby said darkly. He stood up. 'Well, be careful, Agnes.'

'What do you mean?'

'Why, don't take cold, my love, sitting by the water in the night air without a coat. What did you think I meant?'

He patted my shoulder and walked away. But though I waited I didn't hear his gate creak. After a few minutes I got up to go home; not through the iron posts, but turning right at the gas lamp, past the row of weather-board cottages that faces the Promenade, where the bird hangs in its cage by the door, next to the hollyhocks; quite the old maritime print. Naturally, the bird had been taken in for the night, but the hollyhocks bloomed on through the summer, nearly reaching the roofs, buds at the top of the spike, blooms in the middle and at the bottom those seed boxes shaped like miniature shortcakes which from childhood I'd loved to pick. Under cover of darkness and in the absence of the owner, I availed myself of this simple pleasure.

'Hullo,' said a voice behind me. 'Sorry, did I make you jump?'

It was Hedley. Certainly he meant to startle me.

'I've been looking for you,' he went on. 'Tubby was telling me—'

'That I'm an illegitimate orphan,' I said into his hesitation.

'Yes. I'm sorry. I didn't know, I didn't mean to hurt you.'

He had his back to the lamp. His cigarette glowed in the shadow. He was holding something against his chest, I could see luminous watch hands. 'Have you still got that kitten?' I said.

'Tubby threatened to throw it in the river.'

'You didn't believe him? He is a cunning devil. You'll have a job to get him to take it back, he'll tell Carole it's disposed of.'

'Then I'll have to keep it.'

'Fellowes won't be pleased if it makes puddles in your room.'

The pale hands of the watch moved with his wrist as he stroked the cat.

'Was it reasonable, not too bad, at the orphanage?'

'It was ugly. That was the worst, once you were old enough to realize it.' It must have been the warm night, apt for confidences, that made me go on. 'They had this seemingly inexhaustible stock of cheap wallpaper, some surplus dumped on them in the thirties, probably as a righteous act of charity. Geometrical designs and tarnished gilt on every wall. The same with clothes. They tried to make them bright yet keep them cheap. So they succeeded in making us hideous. It didn't matter till other girls asked you home and you saw *their* walls and *their* dresses. After about fifteen. From then to eighteen was my worst time.'

'You stayed late.'

'I was still at school. No one stands in your way these days. They see the promising Redbrick scholar gets her place.'

'And her grant?'

'Yes, but in any case someone—I had money left me then.'

'Conscience money?'

'How quick you are.'

A spy. A brain washer. An intelligence agent.

'Did you have to look after the young ones?'

'Yes, and help about generally. They didn't make slaves of us. We were lucky. It was a *good* home, you know. Genuine orphans from respectable families. I was the only one who was a bit—tainted.'

'Someone used influence to get you in?'

'Probably. I was paid for. That is, contributions were made. I don't suppose they covered the whole cost of keeping me there.'

'What were they like, the people in charge?'

'Matron? Not too bad. She hated you to snivel.' I found myself staring at the ground in the darkness, seeing nothing, instinctively reacting to a memory.

'Did you have enough to eat?' he said.

'I'm alive. There was the war, and afterwards austerity, so it was more or less the same everywhere. They did their best, they really did.'

'Did you have apples? To eat, I mean, not cooked.'

'Yes, quite often. Why ever on earth do you ask?'

'Just that we had some boys from an orphanage at school, twins, Cockneys, God knows how they'd got right up there. And sometimes we'd bring apples with us—'

'When you were well off!'

'No, no, on the way we had to pass a house with a garden. There weren't many. They had two fruit trees and a low wall. Anyway we used to eat the apples in break. Those Cockneys,

I'll never forget them, watching every bite. And when we'd finished they used to say: "Give us the core, mate!"'

'And did you?'

'Sometimes.' He was silent a minute. 'When shall we start these driving lessons?'

'You don't have to make up to me for being an orphan.'

'I know that. Have the control fitted.'

The scent of stocks and roses from Tubby's garden came to me on a current of air. Across the river I could see the red lights on the power-house chimneys. Be careful, Agnes.

'All right,' I said. 'Do you specially want to keep that kitten? If not I will.'

'Perhaps that would be best. Take it, then.'

The warm fur cushion immediately set up a wailing mew. Poor pussy mittens, I don't blame you, so should I cry if I were torn away like that: such were my unvarnished thoughts as I thanked him and said good night.

I walked along the unlit path between the river wall and the back yards of the street. Already there were lights in many bedrooms, coloured squares of drawn curtain: the village goes early to bed. I turned up the alley by the pier. Two men stood against the dim light of the street. I hesitated, but they were only talking, and what they were saying I need not hear. Then as I approached I recognized Tubby's voice, unusually subdued.

'It's going to cost a hell of a lot. I'll see what I can do. But it's her money that gets us the extras, for what they're worth.'

The other man was Tom. I came up with them.

'No wonder I didn't hear your gate creak, Tub,' I said. 'I suppose you haven't been in yet.'

They looked at me blankly for a moment. Then Tubby recovered himself.

'I saw Tom in the street and went to speak to him.'

I held out the kitten. 'I'm taking over the tail-less wonder.'

'That's a relief. I gather you begged it from its protector. Well, good night. I'll see you tomorrow, Tom.'

It was an awkward hasty departure, lacking Tubby's usual *panache.*

Tom and I walked up the street. He hadn't spoken. 'You don't mind about the kitten, do you?' I said, as we turned into the gap between the houses. 'I don't think it will cost much to keep.'

'Of course I don't mind.'

We walked into the levelled space that had been the floor of a chalk-pit, towards the cottage that once belonged to the manager and now was ours.

Tom cleared his throat. 'Tubby was thinking of painting his house,' he said.

I made no reply. We had been married six years. I knew by now when Tom was telling a lie.

That was my first intimation that something was wrong; the first nebulous unfocused question.

I can see now the significance of what had gone before, and what followed; those surface-simple evenings in The Ship, the trivial incidents of long warm days, barely perceptible ripples in our backwater: I see their relevance now. But at the time I was asleep.

Chapter Five

Not that Tubby's house didn't need new paint; the window frames were cracked from exposure to the dust, squalls, and salt winds of the estuary.

We were all there a few evenings later. Wednesday, it must have been, after Tom's lecture at the museum, which we all attended, even Hedley.

Tom was having the car serviced; Hedley took him, and Tubby the rest of us. To my inexpressible chagrin the pleasure of returning in what Tubby called Hedley's firecracker fell to Carole; she went ahead to make coffee. So when I arrived he was already sitting in an armchair that had been pounded by the fights of the boys and torn by the claws of the Abyssinians.

I went straight to the bottles set out on the table; its surface bore the scorch marks of hot plates like so many moons.

'What's the matter?' Hedley said, abandoning his attempt to reach the drink before me.

I poured myself a large Scotch. 'Life is black and futile.'

'Shine in your husband's glory,' he said coolly, refilling his glass. 'It was a good lecture.'

The importance of the estuary in Roman Britain. The roads, the camps, the depots, the settlements; the temple outside Shayle; the mosaic pavement half preserved alongside Flour Lane, which was once Floor Lane, in ploughed fields where the furrows were speckled with small white cubes that had formed pictured gods for Romans to walk on. Yes, it was a good lecture, Tom knew it all. If only he wouldn't say declivity when he meant slope.

'A lot of people came,' said Hedley.

'Shayle is culture-conscious. They have a college. I went there. So did Tom. That's where we met. Only he was postgrad and I was a simple second-class skillet. Two Shayle alumni.' I swallowed half an inch of whisky. 'Anyway it's a good museum. Limited but interesting. Quite pleasant to wander round before the lecture. Tom's improved it. Five years ago it was a mess. Narwhals and seventy-fours and flint arrowheads—all flung together anyhow. He chivvies the governors, makes them paint the place, invites good people to talk.'

The Stavesacre Foundation Museum of Maritime History and Natural Science: as most often known, Shayle Museum. Tom was deputy curator; when Stover retired he would be curator. It was his ambition and his life.

The men came in. They'd gone straight to the attics for a quick glance at the experiments, much as Helen had gone into her house to glance at Malcolm, to make sure he was safe in bed as she'd left him. I suppose I should have offered to help Carole in the kitchen; but I ate with better appetite in that house if I didn't positively know that a dog had lain on the tea towel or a cat licked the butter.

Hedley repeated his praise to Tom. Helen joined us.

'All right?' Ian asked her.

She pursed her cheeks in the mechanical half smile she never had time to develop. 'Fast asleep. Of course he's old enough now to be left. He wasn't very keen, but he's got to start sometime.'

'Couldn't you have asked Livia?' I said.

'Livia?' Hedley was astonished.

'She often sits in for Carole,' Helen explained. 'She used to for me, but it wasn't really satisfactory.'

'To whom?' said Hedley. He was too sharp for his own good, it seemed to me.

'She used to tell him ridiculous stories, keep him awake half the night,' said Helen. 'Otherwise she's reasonably trustworthy, no doubt. Of course I'd never leave money about.'

I saw Ian blush for his wife, and was glad that Carole brought in the tray. One thing could be relied on at Tubby's; food and drink. The plates might not bear inspection, but what was on them was good and lavish. What the family left was devoured by the animals.

We were a rather heavy party. Tom was obviously suffering nervous fatigue after the lecture, Ian seemed to have one of the headaches to which he was becoming prone, I was drinking black coffee to counteract the whisky. Helen silently looked me over, reckoning the cost of my haircut and my new shoes. Sometimes I felt suspicion in the way she stared at me; if she had disliked me less she might have said something.

Carole and Tubby kept up the talk between them; she with scatty comments on the lecture which showed that she had only half understood it, he moving among the bird cages, feeding the budgerigars with crumbs of Stilton, telling us the last recorded sight in the area of Montagu's harrier, full of his success in analysing owl pellets.

'What's that?' Hedley said.

'Well my dear chap, you know owls prey on small field creatures, mice and so on. They swallow the tasty morsel whole, digest what they need, then disgorge the bones and fur in little balls. You find these on the ground, and if you pick them apart delicately you can recognize the constituents, discover owls' eating habits. For example I've got a whole field-vole's skull—'

'Tubby!' Carole protested. 'We've just finished eating. Please.'

Tubby looked surprised and injured. 'I thought you'd be interested. Everyone likes playing the detective. Shall we take a turn round the attics then, if you're all ready?'

There was a general move at this suggestion. Hedley stared at the carpet, as if picturing the history of its many stains and splashes.

'Coming?' I said.

He looked up blankly.

'To see the lab,' I explained.

He stood up. 'Sorry. I was thinking of owl pellets.'

'Revolting Tubby. Did it make you queasy?'

'No. Why?'

'You looked rather despondent.'

He shrugged, and paused by the aquarium. 'Needs cleaning,' he said.

I couldn't help glancing round the room, at the paint thick with fingermarks, the good furniture hacked and scraped by toes and heels, the wallpaper scrawled waist-high with generous arabesques in wax crayon: Carole encouraged the children to express themselves.

'Tubby may be collecting the algae,' I said; a lame excuse for Tubby's sake.

'What's that? Algae?' said Tubby himself, darting back. 'Aren't you two coming? If you want to see algae,' he said to Hedley, 'ask Tom to show you his slides under the microscope. The smaller they get, the better they look. Even Agnes thinks they're pretty.'

'What's the use of being pretty if you're invisible to the naked eye?'

'I suppose they're visible to each other,' said Hedley.

'Ah, no go, old man. Algae don't have anything *you'd* recognize as a sex life.' Tubby sighed. 'A trouble-free existence.'

Hedley had nothing to offer on this.

We went round the attics, dutifully admiring trays of dismembered pellets, test tubes, cartons of earth, charts, and graphs that to me were quite meaningless.

'Hasn't Tubby a microscope?' Hedley asked me.

'No, it would be pointless when he can use Tom's. He *does* use it more than Tom, in fact. But then if Tom wants binoculars, he borrows Tubby's, and if either of them want photographs, they ask Ian.'

'All for one and one for all,' he said. 'How long has Tubby known them?'

'Ten years. That's when he came here.' I paused. 'You know Tom's not Ian's brother, only his stepbrother.'

He looked at me with surprise. 'No, I didn't know that.'

'Tom's mother was Ian's father's second wife.' I had to pause to make sure the Scotch hadn't muddled me. 'She was a widow. Tom was five when she remarried.'

'How old was Ian?'

'Eleven.'

Tom must have heard his name. He came across to us.

'I don't know if you want to go home, Agnes,' he said. 'Ian and Tub and I are going out for a bit.'

'You're tired already.'

'Not really. Anyway we shan't be long, just a couple of hours.'

'Can you see in the dark?' Hedley said, not bothering to hide his scepticism.

Tom flushed. 'We're not going to look, we're going to listen for nocturnal migrants. You can hear the flocks' wing beats and hear them calling to each other.'

'Migrants? So early?'

'There's nearly always something on the move from one part to another, not necessarily overseas.'

'In short, as every child knows, birds fly about in the air,' I said.

'Come on, then,' Hedley said. 'I'll walk home with you.'

We said good night to the others and went out together. It was not quite dark. The tide was running out; the boats had swung round on their buoys to face upstream. We walked through the posts, along the silent street.

'I saw your kitten's handsome brothers and sisters this evening,' he said. 'Carole showed me the pedigree forms. Such in-breeding. What you might call incestuous sheets.'

I stared up at the white brick parapet of Woodey's roof. Painted across it in letters two feet high were the words *Ships Provisioned*. All notices faced the river in Gunfleet. The Ship Tavern. Catholic Church. J. W. Ancrum & Sons Ltd.

'Carole was an Ancrum, you know,' I said. 'That used to be the Ancrum house, ever since it was built, till industry made the estuary too dirty for the wealthy to live in. Ancrum's used it as an office, then it was let, and when Carole married they gave it to her. Or she pays a little rent, perhaps, I don't know the details.'

'Don't you think Tubby would pay the rent?'

'Not necessarily. Tubby's not rich.'

'A pathologist needn't starve.'

'He doesn't, you saw that. He spends a lot on food and drink. They have a big car, the four children will have to go to expensive schools, and there's the menagerie to keep up, the experiments, the hobbies. And the turf to follow, as he says.'

'Plus other forms of gambling.'

'What do you mean? What do you know about it?'

'Just what I gathered from things he said when he took me to the hospital.'

'You didn't gather he was in debt, did you?'

'Only that he'd had bad luck lately. Why?'

I told him what I'd overheard between Tubby and Tom, and Tom's unconvincing explanation.

'Poor Carole,' he said.

'Why not poor Tubby, or poor kids?'

'It can't be pleasant to wonder if you were married for your money.'

'I didn't say she—'

'I know you didn't. You can leave uncivilized speculation to me. Let's say that to a gambler, a virtually free house and a substantial bank balance would be fair addition to a woman's natural attractions.'

A sound, a sort of smothered snort, escaped me.

'You don't think she has any natural attractions?' he said.

'I'm no judge,' I murmured, endeavouring to retrieve my lapse.

We walked past the miniature railed basements of the Victorian terrace, pathetic imitations of the areas of the rich. At the end cottage we could see along the side of the house.

Two figures were moving in the dusk among golden rod and a litter of soap-boxes.

'There's Lenny,' Hedley said, 'giving his father a hand with the garden.'

'I didn't think you had such a sentimental mind.'

'No one's more sentimental than me,' he said bitterly. 'Anyway what do you mean?'

'You spoke as if you support the gifted idiot myth. You know, poor dotty Lenny with the wonderful green fingers. He's not giving his father a hand, he's just standing there, getting in the way.'

As we passed the black hulk of the church Father Ryan opened the presbytery door and put out a milk bottle. We exchanged good nights.

'Was that the priest?' Hedley said. 'I didn't think you were one of his flock.'

'Have you ever heard of people saying good night because they're neighbours?'

We turned into the gap that led to the chalk-pit.

'It's a start,' he said. 'You'll get talking to him, and before you know where you are you'll be taking the old splash at the font.'

'Not on your life. Not here, anyway. I looked inside that church once, from curiosity. Heavens, it was so ugly I flew out after half a minute.'

'That's all that matters to you, isn't it?' he said, 'what a thing looks like. Your first criterion. Wallpaper, dresses, churches, people, all the same. If they don't come up to standard, into the dustbin and down with the lid. You'll only accept the best, only be nice to the nice.'

What right had he to stand there moralizing, censuring me left, right, and centre? I was too indignant to answer;

and too upset. If that was what he thought—and that quiet clipped voice was not teasing—that was the impression I had given.

We reached the cottage.

'Your outraged dignity won't let you speak to me now, will it?' he said.

'Oh yes it will. Good night.'

I walked quickly away and opened the kitchen door; we usually lock it when both of us are out, but Tom had forgotten. I closed it behind me.

My character had been judged and found wanting. In his casual analysis there had been no censure; that was my imagination, my reaction. Hedley thought ill of me, that was all; it gave him no concern. But it mattered to me. Alas, alas, it did.

I switched on the light. Ah, Jesus! I was tired of living in that shabby, poky, draughty, lonely cottage.

I forgave him of course, almost forgot it, when he came to tell me the car was ready. He wanted to drive it himself before letting me loose at the wheel; so we went together up to Sankton's in the heat of the afternoon, one Friday. As I was going to be with Hedley, I thought I could safely wear my pink dress, the one Helen disapproved. What I didn't foresee was that he would fetch the car from the sheds while I paid for the fitting. Thus after all I had to suffer Sankton's hypocritical deference, so subtly tainted with mockery.

'I thought you'd passed the test,' he said to me. 'I saw your car parked in Culham some time ago.'

'I've never taken it to Culham.'

'Perhaps your husband borrowed it.'

His eyes quizzed me for reaction. They were startling eyes, shallow, shapely, pale grey against his coffee-coloured skin, with fine black lashes; the eyes of a fast worker.

I handed him the money. 'He's never had it out without me. You must have seen one like it. They're common enough.'

'I suppose so,' he said. 'I'll give you a receipt for this.'

Hedley brought round the car. I sat down beside him and played with the new pedals while more petrol was put in. He glanced about the forecourt, unable to conceal his disappointment.

'It's Livia's half day,' I said.

The blue eyes gave me a freezing look. I was quite glad, incredible thought, that Sankton came. He had change for Hedley and for me a dirty slip of flimsy with some illiterate scribble on the back: my receipt. Such were the standards of Sankton's garage.

I couldn't believe we were in the same car as I'd guided across the marsh, we moved out so smoothly. He changed gears with one finger, no doubt to show off.

'Where shall we go?' he said.

'Straight on to Culham. I want to do some shopping.'

'What do you propose to do with me? Stand me outside like a dowager's chauffeur?'

'I only want a basket for the cat.'

The chalk verges of the Roman road shot by. I could no longer distinguish their bright stunted flowers. After a few minutes we caught up with an open truck loaded with workmen, most of them half-stripped, brown as Arabs.

'Don't pass,' I said.

'I've been driving twenty-five years without so much as scraping the paint.'

I hadn't been afraid: but after his sermon I wasn't disposed to say: *he's so handsome, let me look.*

He was the youngest workman, sitting at the back of the truck, staring vacantly at the hedge. He wore the usual filthy cap over a shock of straight hair, and a silver chain round his neck, so long that the medal or charm or locket it carried was hidden in the hairs of his chest. How vain they are, and how conscious of what they're doing, the navvies with their chains and the Hedleys with their watches.

We passed the truck. I looked my last. He reminded me of the electrician's mate; or what the electrician's mate had been. I could never remember that he would have changed, always saw him as he was ten years before, the tall blue-eyed boy who carried the tool bag for mending fuses at the orphanage, who left his master to smoke over tea in the kitchen and came running up to the linen store where we met in passionate embraces, to whom ultimately in the same linen store I yielded my inestimable treasure, virginity. And short work he made of it; had to, for fear of matron.

'What are you thinking?' he said.

'How well you drive.' Tubby would have launched a psychological exposition on the ease with which that sprang to my lips. 'When did you start?'

'You want to work out my age, don't you? I'll save you the trouble, I'm nearly forty-six. Old enough to be your father, with a few years to spare.'

There was more matter for Tubby. 'You don't know how old I am,' I said.

'Do *you,* exactly?'

'Twenty-seven, two months, three days. I wasn't left in a basket, I was born in Shayle hospital, all proper, apart from one trifling circumstance. I didn't go in the orphanage till my mother died.'

'Can you remember her?'

'I was only two. I know what matron told me, she came from Yorkshire and was well spoken. She probably never even told them her real name.'

'And no one adopted you.'

'I was rather old. Most people like to take a child from a few months. Besides—' I had to stop. Even now the thought of it sent me into a nervous tremble. 'I used to squint.'

'Did it correct itself, in time?' he asked, after a minute.

'No, someone paid for the operation. More conscience money, as you call it.'

'From your father? Or your mother's people?'

'How should I know? It was all done through solicitors.'

'But haven't you ever tried to find out?'

'No,' I said abruptly, 'I didn't want to know. I didn't care.'

He made no comment. That was as well. Through my carelessness I was suddenly sailing tricky reaches.

We had reached the outskirts of Culham; wastes of cemeteries, asylums with yellow brick walls, row on row of semi-detached houses faintly greyed with chalk, gimcrack shopping parades and an occasional depressed pub. Behind every major bus stop stood a concrete lavatory.

'Look at it,' I said, 'the architecture of contempt. Here, scum, this is good enough for you. No one who works or lives or was born in the estuary can possibly have any sensibility. The estuary! I hate it.'

He changed down soberly behind a bus. We were approaching the centre of Culham, with its narrow streets of vulgar shops. 'Where do you want to get this basket?' he said. 'And what do we do about parking?'

In the end we stopped in the car park behind the cinema. He came with me to buy the basket; then he went to the post office. I was standing outside the chemist's trying to subdue my guilt at having bought a lipstick that I wanted but didn't need, when I saw Ian come out of a door a few yards along the road: Stenlock's, the solicitors. Hedley was not in sight; but I was glad he hadn't wheedled more out of me.

I ran up to Ian. 'Hullo,' I said, 'what are you doing?'

He turned round so quickly he nearly knocked me down.

'I'm sorry,' I said, seeing how I'd startled him. 'I was so surprised to see you.'

'Oh, yes, of course,' he said. 'Tubby couldn't make it this afternoon.'

'But you can play golf on your own.'

'Well yes, but I don't care to. I've been doing various odds and ends.'

I'd never seen Ian and Hedley together alone; always Tubby had been present, or Tom, or both.

'Shall we have some tea?' I said. 'Fair shares.'

His sudden smile made brightness well in his eyes like tears. He glanced at his watch. 'All right, Ag. Only let's be quick.'

We had to walk past the post office to reach Culham's only tolerable tea shops. Hedley came out on the steps as we approached.

Ian held me back. 'Look.'

'Hedley? I know, he brought me in. I was going to fetch him.'

Ian took his hand from my arm. 'You didn't say so.'

'Don't you like him?' I said stupidly.

He looked at me, frowning, and seemed about to say something; but changed his mind and turned away.

Hedley of course hadn't failed to see and join us.

'We were going to have tea,' I said, blurting out what was in my mind; realizing a second later that Ian was now more or less bound to us. If I'd had the sense to keep my mouth shut he'd have had a chance to leave. 'Will you come?' I asked Hedley: I couldn't tell him to wait till we'd finished.

'Yes, if you want me to,' he said.

I had wanted it a few moments earlier.

'Where shall we go then?' I said unhappily. 'The Willow's nearer.'

'No, the Willow has those hideous murals,' Ian said quickly. 'Let's go on to Powlett's.'

It was quite a long walk. Hedley asked, in his inquisitive way, what had happened to Tubby. I was surprised that he remembered their Friday arrangement. Ian explained rather shortly.

'I thought you were the one who was to be too busy to come this week,' Hedley said. 'Catching up with the budget.'

'There was less than I thought.'

I exerted myself to speak.

'Tubby might have given you a ring. It would have saved you coming all the way to Culham.'

Ian looked uncomfortable. 'He couldn't help it. They wanted him to do something at the last minute. He met me where he usually picks me up, then had to fly off again.'

'What did you do with your clubs?' Hedley asked.

'I keep them in the boot of Tubby's car. We both do.'

We entered Powlett's, Ian in his grey suit, Hedley in the shabby shirt and flannels, I in the pink dress that Helen considered fast, and sat down to be waited on. I did not expect much felicity from the next quarter of an hour.

It wasn't as bad as I'd feared. Hedley continued to ask

innocuous questions about Culham Park: was it a public course, how many yards, and so on. Ian continued to answer shortly as was consistent with politeness. He was very fond of Tom. Perhaps he thought I was failing in my duty to flit about Culham with another man: he himself was exempt on grounds of relationship. If only he could have seen the complete indifference with which Tom had received my proposal to practise driving with Hedley. I think Hedley himself was rather shaken.

There was a rash of streaks on the back of my hand, shaded from pink to red, where I'd tested lipsticks. I fished in my handbag for paper tissues, and found a shred right at the bottom. I cleaned my hand with it as best I could, then set about returning all the rubbish I'd had to pull out; purse, compact, diary, cologne, and so on. At the end a grubby scrap of paper lay on the table, scrawled with an address in soft blunt pencil, 28 Dyer St., Culham. Ian was staring at it in amazement, as well he might; I couldn't think how such a thing had come into my possession.

'What's that?' I said, turning it over.

'Sankton gave it to you,' said Hedley.

'Of course, the receipt. Just like him. Grubby and opportunist.'

I caught a glint from Hedley's eyes that I was beginning to recognize and fear.

'He's a good-looking lad,' he said.

Ian glanced at his watch. 'I must go.'

He signed to the waitress, and took some small change from his pocket, looking for a coin to leave on the table. Hedley stretched out his hand, the left hand, with the masculine watch round the masculine wrist. He shifted the sugar bowl, which none of us had moved. Underneath lay a shilling from some previous customer. He must have seen the unevenness of the bowl.

'Ah, good fellow,' Ian said with a smile. It was his first moment of ease. He pushed the bowl back over the shilling.

'Ian! You're not going to leave it there?'

'Well you can't take it with you, Ag.'

All his quick charm came into that tease. I could have wept. I turned my face away from him. Hedley's blue eyes looked right into mine. I stood up, and made my way out.

Helen. It was Helen, with her squalid economies, her pennyturning closeness, she was infecting him, Ian, my Ian, generous, charming, honest, and conscientious.

They came out together. Ian looked as if he didn't know whether to laugh or be penitent.

'What's the matter?' he said. 'You didn't really think I'd deprive the poor girl of her due?'

'All right,' I said. 'Here's my share.'

'Don't be silly.'

'But you agreed before we came.'

'To have tea. I made private reservations. Don't argue, Ag, and be less credulous of men.'

Perhaps he meant that as a shaft: I was too mortified to care. I'd more or less forced two men to give me tea they would never have stopped for themselves; I hadn't even enjoyed it, such was my nervous fear of their disagreeing.

'Are you still angry with me?' Ian said, teasing.

'No. I never was.'

'She's angry with herself,' said Hedley.

'Do you pride yourself on your understanding of women?' Ian retorted.

Don't let them start sniping, I thought, as Hedley paused

in surprise. And then, incredible joy, Tubby, saviour Tubby came round the corner of Herne Street.

I rushed to meet him, never questioning his timely appearance, thinking only that it would heal all breaches.

'Tubby!' I called: and felt like a smack in the ribs the shutter of annoyance that flicked across his face. It was too late to turn back. I stood still: and as he came up to me his face resumed its usual bland mask.

'Agnes, my sweet, why are you scurrying to my protection? What rude dastard has assaulted you?' He caught sight of Ian and Hedley. I shrank from the expected quip about guilty men, but it didn't come, perhaps because Tubby himself was bored with fatuous pleasantries.

'Quite a gathering of Gunfleet,' he observed. 'Ian, I'm so sorry if I've made you wait. I was held up.'

'It's all right, Tub,' Ian said hastily. 'I was explaining to them that you'd been called away.'

There seemed to be a fault in logic somewhere; but I couldn't place it, partly because my brain isn't logical and partly because Tubby was wondering aloud whether they had time to go up to the golf course. Finally they decided to go home, and we parted; they went off to wherever Tubby had left the Jag, Hedley and I to the car park.

'Will you drive back?' he said.

'Please don't make me start in traffic.'

'Start? I thought you could drive?'

'I meant start with you.'

'You'll have to face traffic with a stranger when you take the test. All right, I'll drive.'

I put the cat basket on the back seat and sat down beside him.

'I'd like to see Tubby and Ian on the golf course,' he said. 'It must be a rare sight.'

'What do you mean?'

'I've never seen anyone play in a lounge suit.'

'Ever heard of a changing room?'

'I suppose so.'

We moved out of the car park.

'Could I take it out this evening?' I said.

'I'm going to London this evening.'

It startled me to be reminded that he had an existence independent of Gunfleet. 'You won't get back till the small hours. Has Fellowes given you a key?'

'I'll stay overnight. Will you be free tomorrow afternoon?'

'Yes, if you're not too tired.'

We turned into the main road, and I exclaimed at the length of the bus queues. It wasn't yet half past four; there must have been some cancellations. We passed the queue for Shayle, and in the middle of it were Tubby and Ian.

'Hedley, stop,' I said quickly, amazed as I was. 'There's Tubby and Ian waiting for the bus.'

'I know,' he said, driving on, 'I saw them. If they'd wanted to come with us they'd have said so.'

'They might not have liked to ask. They must have seen us, do go back.'

'Show me how to make two turns in this traffic.'

'You needn't. Go round the block to the left.'

'All right. Remember you wanted it.'

I was afraid the bus might have arrived to take them away, but they were still there. Hedley drew in beside them. They stopped talking so suddenly that I doubted whether they'd seen us till that moment. They moved, and behind them was Tom; he'd been hidden by Ian's height, and I had the impression he'd broken off speaking to the man beside him, a workman with a cap pushed on the back of his head, hair curling over his ears, bulging green eyes, the look of an untamed animal, a man familiar to me. Why? Why? Where had I seen him? That and my surprise to see Tom struggled in my head like some high-powered current through the few seconds of their getting into the car. I let Tubby sit in front, as he wisely suggested, gave him the cat basket to hold, and sat in the back, half on Tom's knees.

'What are *you* doing here?' I asked.

'I've just come off the train. I've been to London.'

'What for? You didn't say you were going.'

'Just some business of the museum's,' he said, with slight irritation.

'It isn't your week for the refinery, then,' said Hedley.

I thought of Avon, oil, petrol, garages: and thus I remembered.

'That man in the queue beside you,' I said to Tom. 'Do you know him?'

'He used to work for Avon till they sacked him.'

'What did he do?'

'Oh, pilfering on an ever-increasing scale. And they suspected he passed out tips to more ambitious operators. If ever a tanker went missing their security usually found he'd been seen with shady characters shortly before. Not that it was much use finding out then. I forget what they caught him at in the end, but of course he had to go. I think they were quite sorry.'

'Why?' said Hedley.

'Walter says he was a lovable rogue.'

'He was still a rogue,' Ian said rather severely: the stern captain.

I didn't know whether I should bother to tell them; I thought I might as well.

'He was up at Sankton's the other day.'

'You didn't see him for more than a moment just now,' Tom said, ending a slight pause. 'Are you sure it was the man?'

'Positive.' I touched Hedley's shoulder. 'Didn't you see him too? You were with your car, and he came out of the shed in front of you. On Sunday afternoon.'

'I don't remember. I noticed him in the queue, he's quite striking. If I'd seen him before I'd have recognized him.'

'Well he only looked out for a moment,' I said, cheated of my witness. 'Besides, you were talking to Livia.'

No one had anything to add to the matter. I sat thinking of Hedley's car, and cars in general.

'Tubby,' I said, 'what's wrong with the Jag?'

'Nothing. I didn't take it today. I went on the bus.'

'Why?'

'Novelty. Empathy. Wanted to savour the sensations of those who use public transport. The baron incognito among the humble wights.'

'But Ian, you said Tubby came to pick you up as usual.'

Ian was silent, puzzled perhaps by my question.

'He didn't,' Hedley said quietly. 'He said *Tubby met me where he usually picks me up.* He didn't mention the car, you just assumed that Tubby would be in it.'

'It all sounds a fuss over nothing to me, my dear girl,' said Tubby, 'and rather a bloody bore as well, if you'll forgive my saying so.'

'I don't think I shall. It's your fault. All those owl pellets. They've given me a taste for playing detectives.'

Hedley turned the car off the main road, towards Gunfleet: the first turning, the long slant across the marsh.

We were not to pass Sankton's garage. No one remarked on this, however. No one spoke at all.

Yet it must have been at the end of that lift from Culham when Ian asked us to spend an evening at his house, all of us, including Hedley. No doubt he felt he ought. He rarely invited people home, even us. And if I had lived in that house, I should have shrunk from laying open to friends its rigorous mediocrity. As for Helen, her social activities were chosen so as not to conflict with her parsimony.

She met us as we went in together by the back door. 'Hullo,' she said. 'Just let me get rid of these unhygienic creatures.'

The day's catch of wasps was struggling in a syrup tin. She splashed them with brown disinfectant, topped that with hot water, swilled it about and poured the lot down the outside drain. The bodies were tinted green. I pushed past the others and ran through the house to the living-room. Ian was standing by the window. Malcolm, in pyjamas, was kneeling on the arm of a chair beside him, something Helen would certainly have forbidden.

'Here they come,' Ian said. 'Off to bed, quick.'

Malcolm slid off the chair. 'Will Tom come up and see me?'

He had grey eyes like his father's, and the same heart-melting smile; but his hair was dark, like Helen's.

'I'll ask him,' I said. 'Good night.'

'Good night, Ag.' He skipped away, not in time to save himself from a cuff on the seat from Ian.

'You say it, Dad,' he complained.

'I'm older.' Ian unashamedly fell back on a parent's feeblest retort. 'Say good night properly.'

'Good night, Agnes.' Malcolm turned at the door, safe from either of us. 'Auntie Agnes.'

He flew upstairs, and Ian did no more than smile at me when the others came in.

We separated at once into two groups, as we always did at first, the men gathering round the projector which Ian had set up to show his latest transparencies. Yet they needed no toy to draw them together, they were already friendly, enviably at ease; whereas Carole, Helen, and I had nothing to distract us from our indifference, contempt, and hostility.

Helen continued a conversation with Carole. 'Did you ask where she'd gone?'

'He said he didn't know.' Carole turned to me. 'Did you know that Livia had left Sankton's?'

'Good heavens! When?'

'On Friday. I went up to see whether she could sit with the children tonight. I've had to ask Mrs Lilley.'

'She didn't say anything to me about intending to change her job,' Helen said. 'I was speaking to her not long ago. I wonder whether she's even told her mother.'

'Why should she?' I said. 'Since her mother's left her to fend for herself a few thousand miles away, I don't see that Livia owes her any duty.'

'A child always has a duty to its parents.'

'Parents start in debt for having brought the child into the world.'

'You're hardly qualified to discuss children.'

'Which is better, not to have them, or to have them and look on them as an economic nuisance?'

'In any case your views are bound to be warped.'

It had taken us about a minute to sink to this level. The

rejoinder that was in my mind would have caused a rupture between the two households. I was silent.

The men had stopped talking. I knew they were listening, unwilling to plunge into the witches' cauldron. However, Hedley came across to us. He was probably no braver, no less loth; but at least he was free to leave Gunfleet altogether whenever he wished.

'What are you talking about?' he asked, smiling with candid malice.

I gave him a look intended to quell. 'Duty,' I said.

'Why don't you call in the expert?' He turned to Ian.

'Not the tax, the moral obligation.' Though Ian was expert in that too, I reflected.

'Agnes, what big words.' Tubby plucked up courage. 'And what big ideas. Impossible, really.'

'What do you mean, impossible?'

'Oh well, duty, you know. No one could tell you what it is, after all.' He sat down with a sigh. 'As far as I'm concerned, when Bob Tucker sends me down a bit of decaying kidney with orders to get cracking, then it's my duty to crack. Yours is to run a red pencil through the students' essays and write helpful notes in the margin. Tom's is to make the museum ever more alluring. Ian's—Ian's duty is to impose duty.'

He stopped, disheartened perhaps by the task of finding a duty for Hedley and the two women.

'So duty is what you're paid for,' I said.

'Whatever is there for you to do. Get on with it, don't cavil, don't quibble. That, you realize, is my theory, not my practice.'

'I'd never resign my right to cavil. You've a duty to use your reason, to stop and think what you're doing.'

'Theirs not to reason why.'

'I don't agree with that,' said Carole, surprising me by her alliance. '"Theirs but to do and die." You shouldn't let yourself be killed blindly following what someone says is duty. That's the cause of all wars.'

'No,' said Ian. 'Greed, vanity, callousness, economic pressures, social anomalies, sometimes political accidents, those are the causes. You can't blame the concept of duty, that's innocent.'

'Just exploited,' said Hedley.

'Well I think we have a duty to survive.'

'Oh Carole, don't be ridiculous,' I said. 'Survive what? You're as good as dead the second you're conceived. The universal pay as you earn.'

She looked puzzled. Tubby smiled faintly at her. 'In any case, my dear, quite apart from mortality, a large part of the tradition you want to survive in is based on the premise that it's supreme virtue to die for country, liberty, religion, even an idea, and what's more to be prepared to let your children die too.'

'I can't see the point,' she complained. 'You're not there to enjoy liberty if you're dead.'

'Wouldn't you die to preserve liberty or life for your children?' said Ian.

'But how could you be sure they'd get it anyway? You might have died for nothing, after all.'

Hedley turned to Tom. 'How wise. You say nothing, and let the rest of us make fools of ourselves.'

Tom shrugged. 'I don't see the sense of talking about duty in abstract, when it's practical, a contingency. You know soon enough when you meet it, but it's not always straightforward—there are so many considerations, sometimes conflicting.' He stopped, aware that they were surprised by his troubled hesitant speech. I looked at the drab carpet. Tom must have felt the bond of embarrassment that had tightened round both of us. 'I suppose duty is facing each situation as it arises,' he went on, 'doing what's right, what's best all round, I mean for the people concerned in each circumstance, the people who'll be affected by what you do.'

He'd never be able to stick to that, it was impossible; or rather, it wouldn't have the effect he hoped. Tom was always unwilling to hurt, to cause trouble. He'd never have made a surgeon, he couldn't have endured to cure anyone by cutting them open.

'You'd better have the final word on duty,' Hedley said to Ian. 'What is it, apart from two and nine on a gallon of Avon Triple?'

'I don't know,' he said after a moment or two. I don't know.'

'How honest,' Hedley said quietly.

Ian moved back in his chair, turning his head away from us.

'What's wrong with love thy neighbour?' I said quickly, at random.

'Nothing,' Hedley said. 'You've left off the inconvenient first part.'

'Truth, then,' I said. 'Duty is truth, truth duty.' I glanced at Tom.

'Truth in my opinion is grossly overrated,' Tubby said. 'I have an affection for large comfortable lies. They're like club armchairs.' He clicked his cigarette lighter on and off, staring at the flame. 'It's so often more humane to let truth go.'

'We're talking about duty, not expediency,' I said.

'Well, well,' said Tubby, 'anyone who sticks to *love thy*

neighbour won't be doing too badly. It's not so easy, is it, Agnes, my charmer? You know I can't help feeling that parable would have been even more telling if the chap *had* been a neighbour of the Samaritan's, or better still a relation. Say a mother-in-law. Well, Ian, old chap, when are we to see these pictures?'

I was not sorry for the change of subject. We pushed our chairs to the end of the room, for Helen refused to disarrange the furniture merely for the projection of extravagant slides.

So many people now take good photographs, dazzling transparencies. Ian's were still outstanding. It was his one hobby, his only personal expense; and if Tom and Tubby hadn't paid for what he did for them in their own particular interests his occupation, his escape, would have been reduced by two-thirds. He hardly went outside the estuary, but even there he found material. It was unfair, in fact. By isolating and highlighting limited aspects he gave it a spurious glamour. Those effects in common life were submerged in general drabness. But that evening, I remember, most of the slides were close-ups of flowers; so brilliant and so beautiful that I kept asking to see each one again.

The visit closed peacefully enough. Helen brought in coffee. We ate and drank without tension. The food was like the house, neat, thrifty, and insipid. Helen had been a domestic science teacher; I often reflected that having to work within a county borough's rations and budget had permanently cramped her management, hardened her inborn meagreness.

I looked at her as she argued with Carole that it was not necessary to spend more than sixpence on a cake of soap. Her face was brown, netted with fine creases, so was her throat, only redder, coarsened by exposure to all weathers, permanently flushed against the pale sides of her neck. The picture of health.

Carole appealed to me for support. 'I never use soap on my face,' I said, 'only cream and distilled water.'

Helen's bright eyes rested on me with contempt; then she turned aside, addressing herself exclusively to Carole.

The day Helen looked at me with approval I'd feel I'd changed for the worse. Yet often I despised myself. Did my face really merit the care with which it was cherished? Why should I struggle to improve and preserve it? For whom?

I joined my husband and Hedley. Tom was asking him how long he meant to stay in Gunfleet.

'Till the engineers come to build Ancrum's new jetty.'

'I wish you wouldn't go till I've sat the test,' I said.

He smiled. 'Your faith is touching, but there's nowhere to stay. Ancrum's have had the rooms booked for six months.'

I had the impression that Tom was appraising Hedley, for what purpose I couldn't imagine. I went to talk to Ian and Tubby; but after a while I became aware of two pairs of eyes turned with more than casual frequency in my direction: Hedley's and Helen's. I was standing next to Ian. I moved away and drifted about the room alone.

When we left, Tom went up to Tubby's attic to look at the progress of the experiments. Hedley walked back with me.

'So you speak Italian?' he said, without preliminary.

'Not very well. It was my second subject at Harefield.'

'Tubby told me Livia used to come to the cottage for lessons.'

'Oh that. Yes, last year. Her father sent her a present when she was twenty. She took a thought she might go to Italy, get in touch. Poor Livia. She couldn't spell English for a start. It was too much for her. After a bit she gave up. The spirit was willing, and so on.'

'Perhaps she couldn't afford it.'

'You don't think I took money?'

'Why did you do it for her?'

'Why shouldn't I? She asked. God knows how she knew I'd ever learnt. These things get round, I suppose. Besides she was so pleased with that present, it was—quite touching. I mean, I could understand her, wanting this family connexion.' We turned into the chalk-pit. 'I suppose she'll get married, if her parents' example hasn't disillusioned her.'

'You said she hates to be tied.' He put his hand on my elbow, steadying me as my foot turned on a stone. 'I suppose that comes from her mother.'

'And the looks from her father. At least she's bound to be asked.' I stopped at the cottage door. 'And most people say yes, for one reason or another.'

'True,' he said quietly.

We said good night and parted.

I dismissed that evening with hardly a thought, a few hours of idle give and take. Why didn't I wake up, think, listen, really listen? But after all, what would it have told me, then?

Chapter Six

THERE WAS AN EVENING WHEN HEDLEY CAME TO GIVE me a lesson. We were to go to Shayle, so that I should familiarize myself with its streets and corners at a time when there was less traffic. For Shayle was where I should be tested.

We pulled in at Sankton's for petrol. He was there himself, at the pumps; and I saw with surprise that he was talking to Helen. I switched off. The hood was down.

'I couldn't say, madam,' he said: the nuance of rudeness in *madam* was masterly. 'She just told me she'd found a job with better pay. She gave proper notice. The rest wasn't any of my business.'

He walked away, insolence in every muscle of his neat backside. Helen had been probing about Livia, and she'd got a dusty answer. Madam. It was a small point in his favour.

'Hullo,' she said, coming up to us. 'Could you give me a lift to Culham? Malcolm was sick and that's made me late. The bus takes ages.'

We couldn't refuse, since it didn't matter to us where we

went, as she well knew. Hedley and I changed places, and she sat in the back.

'We have a lecture this evening,' she said. 'I don't want to miss the start, but while I'm in Culham I think I'll see Livia. Since this fellow doesn't know what job she's gone to I'll ask her myself.'

'Why do *you* want to know?'

'Someone ought to keep an eye on her. These girls from broken homes who wander about from job to job often end on the streets.'

Rage swelled my throat. I couldn't speak.

'Suppose she's left the district?' said Hedley.

'We'd get in touch with our nearest branch. I must say that's a highly dangerous way to light a cigarette.'

'What's your lecture about?' he said, unperturbed.

'Ways we could help after a nuclear attack. Most of us haven't time to belong to Civil Defence, but we like to know what we could do.'

I gave a short laugh.

'It's exactly people like you who treat these things irresponsibly beforehand and then depend on the ones who've prepared themselves,' she said.

'All experts owe their existence to the ignorant. Anyway what makes you think you'll be in any shape to help others? Ten megatons don't respect uniforms.'

'What's made Malcolm sick, do you think?' Hedley said quickly. 'The heat?'

'No, one of Carole's hamsters got hurt and had to be killed. I told him it would have been cruel to keep it alive, but they don't have the sense to see it at that age. If you take the right fork here we'll avoid the traffic lights, and it brings us nearer the road. Dyer Street. The lane round the back of the Essoldo.'

'Twenty-eight?' I said.

'How did you know?'

'It was on a scrap of paper I got from Sankton. I suppose someone made a note of it in a hurry and lost it.'

'Not this turning,' said Helen.

'It's a short cut,' he said.

'Do you know Culham then?'

'I've been in once or twice.'

We went through the back roads to Dyer Street. A lane, Helen had called it; so it still was, in outline, narrow, curving with houses on one side only, a low terrace of mid-Victorian cottages facing what had once been a patch of common but was now unedifying backs; the blank brick of the Essoldo, with its ventilation shaft and fire escapes, the printing works, the metal works. Twenty-eight was the last house of the terrace, opposite the timber yard; the top ends of long planks were visible over the wall.

'We'll wait,' said Hedley. 'We might as well take you all the way.'

'That's very kind of you.' She positively bloomed under his attention. 'I shan't keep you a minute.'

He was full of consideration for Helen. I hadn't failed to notice him intervene when he thought the fur would start flying.

'Where's Tom this evening?' he said. 'On the marsh?'

'No, he's working late. He won't be in till about nine.'

I caught an odd expression on his face, as if he had heard a joke while his mouth was full of castor oil. It was gone in a second. I saw from the change in his eyes that someone had answered Helen's knock.

I knew the woman by sight. She had frizzy blonde hair, and a pair of sharp eyes in a wolfish face. The door was open only a little. She blocked the space with her body as if she were fending off some salesman. Her replies to Helen seemed brief and unfriendly.

'It's a poor shrine for Livia,' I observed.

'I don't suppose she can afford better.'

I felt a squeeze of guilt. It must have been months since I'd spoken to her beyond a casual greeting. I resolved to mend my neglect.

The woman at the door gave what was obviously a negative and shut the door in Helen's face. Hedley started the car, and I got out to let her in.

'No luck?' he asked. 'She didn't look very amiable.'

'She wasn't,' Helen said grimly. 'Downright rude in fact. Livia's gone, and she says she's no idea where. When I asked her about forwarding letters she said she didn't expect any.'

'Then Livia must have told her mother she was moving,' I couldn't resist pointing out.

'Where's this lecture to take place?' Hedley asked.

'Just drop me at the corner of Marlborough Road, thank you.'

If I'd needed witness to the charm of wide-set pure blue eyes Helen's expansiveness would have furnished it.

There wasn't room to turn, even in my car. He had to drive on. Beyond the house the road took a sharp bend to the left. It was like being in prison; nothing but brick. On the right the wall of the timber yard, on the left the wall of the garden hardly enlivened by a dingy green door, and immediately beyond it the arch of the railway embankment under which the road ran.

'I think I've seen that woman before,' Helen said.

'She works on the stocking counter at Denning's.'

'That accounts for it. Of course I don't buy stockings as often as you do.'

Beyond the arch the lane swung round to join Herne Street.

'If you turn left it's the third along,' said Helen. 'She'd need to be more polite to customers than she was to me. I asked if she'd got anyone to take the room, because there's a Swiss girl at the hostel who'd like to move out. She was most offensive—said she was going on holiday next month and didn't want any foreigners in the place while she wasn't there. You know, I had the impression that she isn't entirely honest. However, here we are. Don't turn, it's only a few yards down the road.'

I got out, tipped up the seat to let her by, and sat back.

'Many thanks.' She leaned down, looking at Hedley; though it was my car, damn it all. 'Oh, a wasp. Filthy things. Dreadful germ-carriers.'

It was on the white panel, drugged with warmth. She whipped a tissue out of the rack by my knees and crushed it. The faint crunch made my teeth clench and my toes curl. At least she wiped away the remains; all but a smear.

'Well, good-bye,' she said. 'Have a good lesson. I'll tell you what I learn in the lecture. It might be useful.'

'The wish is father to the thought,' I said as she walked away. 'Just think how she'd love it—all the feckless irresponsible slobs helplessly crusted with burns, unable to move out of range of being bossed.'

'What's the matter with you?' he said sharply. 'You'd be lining up for tea and bandages with everyone else, only too grateful.'

'I suppose Livia's meant to be grateful for their efforts to keep her from prostitution. What minds, they make me sick. It's all they can think of.'

'I expect they're wise by experience.'

'How do they think they could stop her? *Keep an eye on her.* What would that do but let them watch it happen? I suppose they'd have the satisfaction of their prediction coming right.'

'They could make sure she has somewhere to sleep. That's often all that turns them to it, girls alone in a strange city, just the need to find a bed for the night. And then they get the habit. Don't you know that?'

'Girls! Must you join in too? It infuriates me, this attitude—she's *a girl.* As if to say an animal, dumb sexual bait. Oh, but I know it's not just because she's a *girl* that Livia gets the treatment. I'll tell you why. Two words, Helen used them. Broken homes. Just let anything be wrong with your family background and you've had it, there's a national network of bosses and busybodies that will mentally clap you in an institution, and there you are, subnormal, semi-delinquent, numb in brain and senses, tabbed, warded, and expected to lick their hands in gratitude for hard beds and gruel.'

My voice had thickened. And the minute I stopped I wasn't angry, only miserable because I hadn't stopped sooner.

All I could do was sink myself in his opinion, already low. How could I say to him: *I don't mean half what I say.* Why should I claim exemption from restraint on account of my petty goads? When compared with millions I didn't know what it was to suffer.

He lit a cigarette and tapped me on the shoulder.

'Come on, orphan Aggie. Change places. And don't forget to look in the mirror.'

When was it that I walked out on the flood wall? An afternoon. The tide was low, exposing the old wall, a curve of huge knobbed flints, dark with slime and weed. I had the kitten on a leash, and half way to the paper mills I sat down on the wall, stroking him, kissing his head, and generally acting soft. That must have been why I didn't hear Hedley come, or see him till I happened to look round; and there he was, standing on the path. The poor cat nearly shot in the river, I jumped so violently.

'I suppose you wanted to watch the show,' I said mortified. 'Have you been walking?'

'Didn't you see the car down there? I thought I'd take a look at these marvellous marshes.'

The white car was drawn up beside a ditch. I hadn't noticed it as I came, absorbed in the kitten and in my thoughts; besides it was not unusual to see a car inexplicably parked on the marsh, belonging to men from the river board or the cable company that built and maintained the pylons or simply to a bird watcher.

He sat down beside me. 'You've chosen a charming spot for a rest.'

Behind us lay a pan of caked mud, broken by half-sunk lumps of timber. Still, there was a white sail on the river, and the sun was shining on the aluminium skins of the oil storage tanks on the far shore, property of Avon's deadliest rival.

'This is your husband's day for the refinery, isn't it?'

I thought. 'Yes. Why?'

'It must be two months since I came. What exactly does he do there?'

'An ecological survey. General effect of the refinery on its site, changes in the shore line, effects of drainage on the marsh, what plants have gone and what established themselves, how the birds have been affected, everything.' I balanced the kitten on my knees. 'The geography department of the University wanted to take charge of the project, but in the end Tom was preferred. Jubilation at the museum, who scent a fat Avon endowment.'

'Will they get it?'

'I expect so. For Avon it's only a tax evasion. Tom's bound to cover himself and them with glory. He knows the estuary like the back of his hand, he's never left it, except for National Service.'

'He wasn't born here.'

'No, but he came very early. To Shayle first, because Ian's father had moved there from Gunfleet. Ian's house was his, he left it to him.'

'What was he, Ian's father?'

'A civil engineer.'

He nodded. 'I saw Tom and Ian setting off for Shayle this morning. Do they always travel to work together?'

'Yes. They share petrol.' I was anxious to dispel any misunderstanding that might have lingered after the episode of the shilling under the sugar bowl. All the same, I wished Tom hadn't been able to give lifts to Ian; while he did so, Ian's chances of getting a car of his own were negligible. Helen could see no need for it.

'Where does Tom come from?'

'Yorkshire.'

'Not a trace left in his voice, is there?'

'He's been here since he was five, twenty-seven years. This kitten's longing to come to you, do you mind?'

He patted his thigh and the kitten leapt across, ecstatically thrusting its head into his arm.

'What do you call it?'

'Mittens.'

'It hasn't any.'

'I know, but I just—' I put out my hand and stroked it.

'What's the matter?' he said, so quietly that I wasn't sure I'd heard right, and had to look at him, doubting. His eyes were steady, expectant, almost pained, I thought, then dismissed it as too unlikely.

'Tom's going to let the caravan. He says we can't afford a holiday.'

That was what I'd been thinking over. He'd drawn it out of me simply by asking, by looking.

He turned away from me, to the river. 'Are you very disappointed?'

'No, not really. But I can't think *why* he's letting it.'

'I suppose he's short of money if he says so. Why don't you sell the car?'

'No. No, I couldn't. Besides he wouldn't take money from me. It's mine, remember.'

'You could try him.'

He was playing softly with the kitten's ears, folding them down in spaniel flaps. Its eyes were closed, it was purring. 'Wouldn't you have been glad to get away from the estuary you hate so much?'

How could I explain, without telling him everything?

'It isn't fair to ask you,' he went on quietly, 'I know what it is. You don't have to say. I'm not blind.'

I was speechless, frozen, my eyes fixed to a cluster of boats moored to a buoy, with ropes swagged over their sides like seaweed.

'Why did you marry him?'

That was what he'd seen. Not all, but enough. How did he know? Was I so careless, so callous, that any stranger of two months could read our life?

He put the kitten in my lap. 'You didn't count on a question like that, I suppose.' He went to stand up.

'Don't go,' I said quickly. 'It isn't that I mind. It's just not easy. Please don't go.'

He sat back. 'Well then, why did you?'

'He asked me.'

'It's usual. Why did you say yes?'

'Because he was—nice. I told you we met at Harefield, that's the Hall, the University. Our paths crossed in a historical society. He'd come back after the army to do his thesis. Only about that time I'd—well, there was a man—'

'You might as well go on.'

'You don't want to hear the banal course of the affair, only the end. When I'd really wrapped myself up in him, he left, got another job. He wouldn't tell me where, but before he said good-bye he did tell me he was married.'

'Would it have stopped you?'

'Thou shalt not steal. I draw the line. If I'd known—well, I didn't, that was that. I can look back now and smile at my green illusions and say quite glibly that it was my own fault. But at the time—'

'It hurt.'

Hurt. I remembered nights of weeping, blank weeks of exhaustion and the will-power of a dead leaf helplessly blown among the splinters. Hurt. It half killed me.

But that was an admission Hedley would not wring from me. He must have inflicted it on some luckless female, several, doubtless, broken their hearts with his short speech and fugitive gentleness, his eyes, mouth, hands, shoulders, the lot, the sum total of Hedley, six foot of intelligent masculinity: who could have withstood it?

'I suppose at this critical moment Tom asked you,' he said.

'You see, I'd made up my mind I wouldn't go through it again, that I was finished with men—well no, sex—'

'That's a bright thing to swear on the eve of marriage.'

'You know what I mean. And there was Tom, so steady, *asking* me. Peace, quiet, security, all within reach.'

'Poor Tom.'

'But I never meant to take all and give nothing.' I was silent a minute. 'What made you ask? Do I behave badly?'

'You don't behave at all, either of you. That's what I noticed. Not constraint, not coldness. As if each were trying to obliterate the relationship to the other.'

How dangerous he was, the candid blue-eyed man.

'Then you must see why I'm not overwhelmed by losing our holiday.'

I'd dreaded it, so had Tom, I knew that: dreaded the ordeal of being confined so close for two weeks, maintaining that scrupulous studied formality with which we fenced round the things that Hedley, for all his acuteness, didn't know.

'How could you do it?' he said. 'How could you think it would work? No one expects love to last, but it gives you a bit of a start.'

'I did love him.'

If only I could have said, I *do.* I couldn't, however. Not though Tom kept me, patient, uncomplaining, never rebuked my extravagances, nursed me when I had flu, not though it had worked well enough for a time, our marriage, before the complications I didn't want to think of.

'Perhaps it wasn't love,' I said, 'what I can't help thinking of as love in spite of all they say. But then they say quiet feelings are a better foundation for marriage than some violent infatuation—'

'They, they. Who are they? Did you really rule your life by some fatuous pulp ethic?'

Tom, poor Tom, he hadn't deserved any of it. There was something childish about him. I remembered him on our honeymoon in the seaside town, turning to me with such bright-eyed eagerness: *shall we get a beach ball, Agnes?* We had, of course, even played with it self-consciously; it was still in the cottage somewhere, at the back of a drawer, cold, flat, and probably perished.

'I was fond of him,' I said, 'I really was. He was sweet and affectionate and playful.'

'What did you marry, a puppy?'

I scrambled to my feet. 'You tripe-eating savage,' I said. 'Do you think you can say what you like to me?'

I turned and ran along the wall, hearing after a minute the echo of my ludicrous outburst, but stifling my shame. Then I remembered the kitten. Humiliating as it would be, I should have to go back. I turned round, and nearly dropped. He was standing a few yards behind me, holding the cat. I'd never known anyone move so silently as he did.

Surprise had got me over the difficulty of looking him in the face, but I had to do the unpalatable rest.

'I'm sorry,' I said. 'I didn't mean it.'

'Nor did I. At least, not the way I think you took it. If that's any consolation.'

'I suppose it is, just a degree.'

'Do you want to walk? Or shall I drive you back?'

'I think I'll walk. Mittens might be frightened in a car.'

He handed me the cat. 'There's something I wanted to tell you,' he said. 'I'm not leaving when the engineers come.'

I had to look down quickly, in case he should see how my spirits lifted.

'You don't look overjoyed to hear it,' he said.

'You know I'm pleased. You'll be able to give me lessons right up to the test.' I could control my face well enough to look at him.

He smiled slightly. 'Yes, but you don't know at what cost. I'm afraid you're not going to like it.' The wide blue eyes met mine without faltering. 'The tripe-eating savage is coming to live in your caravan.'

'Why?' I asked Tom.

'I'd sooner let it to someone we know.'

'What do we know about him? Practically nothing.'

'I should think we could trust Walter's recommendation. Oh, he's a decent chap.' He turned the pages of the annual bird report that had come by the morning post. 'I didn't think you'd mind, Agnes, I'm sorry. I thought you liked him quite well.'

'I do.'

'You're happy about the driving, aren't you?' He looked up. 'Are you?'

I went hot for a multitude of causes. 'Yes. Absolutely. I *don't* mind about the caravan. It's just that I can't think why he's taking it.'

'He said he didn't want to leave Gunfleet yet.'

'But why? *Why*?'

It was pointless to ask Tom, he couldn't tell me; and the only person who could I didn't want to ask.

Yet in those long hot days I had enough chances, sitting for hours beside him in the car, day after day. Shayle, Shayle, Culham, Shayle—I thought I must know every crossing, every island, every corner of those narrow streets, crowded with shoppers and traffic. What relief, what joy, when he would say: *on the marsh today, pure driving.* We used to go out on the Level or the Reach to practise stopping and reversing and slipping the clutch.

Once we turned off the main road by the cement works between Gunfleet and Shayle, where the hill curves down to the marsh like a causeway between two vast pits. He made me stop half way down. The chimneys towered out of space, toppling against the maritime clouds. The grass bank was bushy with valerian and lucerne, pastel ghosts of red and purple flowers, without a shred of green, a single summer's growth bleached as if by some galactic ray. Grey blobs were strung along the wire fence like wool caught from sheep, but it was dust trapped and coagulated round the barbs. Against the quiet humming of belts and extractors in the works I told him about the electrician's mate.

I don't know what prompted me, but out it all poured, one great self-indulgent wallow: the uproar when we were found out, the ghastly half-hour in matron's office, the unremitting supervision, the threats of being taken from school, the dread of losing my chance to heave myself out of institutions by way of Harefield—pitiful notion as I now see it to have been, but at the time the height of my ambition. Poor Hedley. How patiently he listened.

'Did you tell Tom?' he asked, when I'd finished.

'Yes. That, and the other one. I thought he ought to know before he committed himself, in case it made a difference.'

'Evidently it didn't.'

A workman was pushing his bike up the hill; its tyres were white with dust. The sun caught glints of silver high above the river: cables slung between the colossal pylons on each bank.

He lit a cigarette. 'Do you notice that smell in the air? I imagine it must be blown upriver from the refinery. It reminds me of a revolting emulsion my mother used to force down my neck when I had a cough.'

He began to tell me about his family, his childhood in the Depression, on another riverside blackened and polluted by industry, far away up the country from the one we overlooked; how he had gone with his father, and other men from the idle yards, walking down to the river mouth where they trapped seagulls to take home to be cooked. How strange it was, to me, to hear someone talk so easily of mother and father and brothers. How close they had been, all of them knit together; and then, so early and so quickly, one after the other dying or being killed, leaving him alone in his twenties.

What made him tell me? Perhaps it was a return for my confidences; or to show me that on the whole I'd been let off lightly.

We got into the habit of stopping to talk; in theory I was taking a rest. Yet at the cottage I hardly spoke to him, hardly saw him, even though he was living only fifty yards away. He used to fetch water from our kitchen and bath in our bathroom, which was downstairs, before we were up in the morning. Yet he never left a trace of his presence, never once forgot soap or towel. He was nothing more than the sound of water running from a tap, or the flush of the cistern in the outside lavatory.

Many were the looks I intercepted in the village, among the women in Woodey's. I wanted to shout: *it was Tom who asked him to stay:* not because I cared what they thought but to spite them and frustrate their gloating disapproval.

But I did care about Ian. At first I persuaded myself that

I was imagining his coolness, his withdrawal from us; but in the end I had to accept it. Perhaps it was due to that dislike of Hedley which he had never expressed but which I had detected—or that combined with, or causing, displeasure at the whole situation, or at my driving in particular. Whatever the reason, it hurt me; but there was nothing I could do.

Imperceptibly we drifted apart, in the summer, all of us. The season for activity on the marsh was at its height. Tom was out more than ever; but he was on his own. Ian seemed always busy apart. I hadn't heard of Tubby for weeks. And when did we stop meeting in The Ship? Why?

But this vision, these questions, come now. At the time I didn't see, didn't ask, didn't think. I was asleep, dreaming.

When did the weather break, the long spell of sunshine give way to high grey cloud? It had changed by the day we went out in the morning; the day Helen stopped us, as we turned by The Ship, to ask not a lift but a favour. Ian in extreme absent-mindedness had left his glasses at home, he needed them for reading and writing. Would we take them to him? Naturally we would.

It was cold. A stiff wind slapped and chopped the grey-green river. I wore a mac, Hedley a short navy-blue donkey coat.

When we got to the offices at Shayle he would come up with me, all innocent of Ian's dislike, or regardless of it. Remembering the teashop, I was afraid of their sniping, reluctant to deepen Ian's displeasure by flaunting its cause. But I might have spared my anxiety. Ian was out. The clerk said he wouldn't be long; he'd gone down to Skinner's for a book.

'I'll leave a note.' It was unnecessary, I suppose. Hedley looked at me as if he thought so.

'Skinner's,' he said as I scribbled. 'The second-hand bookshop by the ferry? With a few shoddy so-called antique pots as a sideline?'

'That's right. Skinner's an odd character, makes me think of a hermit crab. They went to school together.'

'That shop has a faintly illicit air.'

'I think it's just neglect. Skinner's too wrapped up in bird-watching to bother. But he gets the men books that are hard to come by, old floras, local histories and so on.'

I took the note and the glasses to the paper-littered desk in Ian's private office, which was the usual cube of grey paint and frosted glass, furnished chiefly with metal filing cabinets; except that on the wall opposite the desk hung a Gauguin print, one sombre naked native girl, lying on her side with her chin on her hand, gazing inscrutably at nothing, lost in a melancholy dream: haunting eyes in a face of luminous shadow.

'Do you like it?' I said to Hedley.

'I've always liked it. As far as I'm concerned he could have thrown the rest away.' He paused. 'There can't be many excise offices with that on the wall.'

It was a good reproduction, well framed. Ian must have paid quite a lot for it. Helen would not have approved, especially in view of the subject. 'What's it called, do you know?' I said. 'Is there a title?'

'Nevermore.'

The clerk looked through the door, anxious for the confidential files. 'Come on,' said Hedley.

We went down the gritty stairs. By the first landing was a window from which, through chinks in the surrounding buildings, the river could be seen. I stopped to stare at that leaden strip which unbelievably rolled to the open sea.

It was only a moment's pause; then I went on. Hedley was on the flight below, and when he heard me coming he waited, his hand resting on the rail. The donkey coat was unfamiliar, I'd never seen him from above. He looked like a stranger. He lifted his face, lined, scarred, prematurely aged by the light grey hair, slightly surprised, as if wondering what kept me; and when he saw me he smiled.

That was when it happened, exactly then, the end of a phase, the mental click as the last strand of my private resistance gave way; when I admitted, looking down at his candid blue eyes: there's nothing I wouldn't do for you, absolutely nothing.

Chapter Seven

Tom's voice went on and on; quiet, monotonous, formal, slightly dogmatic, lecturing us as we trudged across the marsh. A primary salt pan is caused by water from the neap tide trapped by plant hummocks or in a hollow. It stagnates, the soil being of low permeability, and eventually evaporates, leaving a high concentration of salt in the area, which becomes barren. A residual pan is a primary pan partly eroded, rain trickling down the sides having washed the salt to the centre. Compound pans are formed when a swirling neap tide breaks down intervening walls of adjacent primary pans. And channel pans occur along the course of salt water runnels and creeks with insufficient scour to keep them open, so that plants from each bank choke the channel at different points. And by a ravishing coincidence all four kinds of pan could be seen on Culham Long Level.

I shivered in the wind that blew across the flats from the river. The evening sky was a chill unbroken grey, fitting like a lid on the zones of the salt marsh: salicornietum, asteretum, halimionetum, named from the dominant species of plant. It was my own fault. I'd suggested that we come, because I knew it would please Tom; a secret appeasement dictated by guilt. I was not to blame that he'd spoilt it by inviting Hedley, whom I'd deliberately excluded. Besides, it was easier for me to meet him again among the others. At least, there were Tubby and Helen. Carole couldn't come; since Livia's departure she's found it difficult to get anyone to sit with the children. And Ian had a headache.

We walked from the pans to the edge of the marsh, into the salicornietum, crunching over its primitive shoots that stick out of the mud like jointed succulent worms.

'What is this stuff?' Hedley asked. He didn't look absolutely enchanted with it.

'Salicornia, Glasswort.'

'Because it's brittle? Or because it's semi-transparent?'

'They used to use it in glass-making on account of its high soda content,' Tom said. 'And pickle it.'

I shuddered. 'Revolting.'

'Poor thing,' said Hedley. 'Just because it hasn't any flowers.'

'Aha! it has, you know,' said Tubby. 'Minute inconspicuous—'

'Warts.'

'Five pink petals don't make a flower, my dear girl.'

'Don't ask me to put salicornia in the same class as a rose.'

'A flower is the reproductive organs of a plant,' said Tom. 'If it doesn't depend on insects for pollination it won't have needed to evolve a coloured scented perianth to attract them.'

'My dear Tom, save your valuable breath. Your charming but obstinate spouse will never admit what she knows to be scientifically true, namely that all the pretties in life are so much bait towards propagation of the species, sugar for the bird. She puts beauty on a pedestal wreathed with incense. In other words, Agnes, you're a sucker for looks, and that's the truth.'

They all stared at me as I flushed, Helen with her usual contempt, Hedley with a faint smile, Tubby in unwonted sharpness that matched his concluding remark. Only Tom spared me, bending over some lichen-crusted mud.

On the river two Avon barges were passing, brilliant, powerful, wealthy; the top civilian fuel of the age.

'I suppose their refinery's ruined the marsh for you?' Hedley said.

'Not at all, increased its interest,' said Tom; he was a true ecologist. 'People who fulminate about power stations and radar spoiling the coast—they claim to be naturalists, some of them, but they must have more sentiment than science. It's what *happens* that's interesting, observing change, not just sitting tight to gloat on what *is*. Naturalists! They have no faith in nature, they don't seem to understand its strength, its endless power of adaptation. No one preserves this marsh, it looks after itself. The upper levels are inundated in spring, when seedlings most need water to establish themselves and grow, and again in autumn, when the water helps to disperse the seeds. If it *were* planned it couldn't be done better. When we're all nothing, this will still be here, changed perhaps but still the earth and what it supports.' He looked round at us apologetically. 'That's my philosophy, not that you asked to hear it. Life must go on, *does* go on. Just life, things that grow, any things, that's what matters. If we radiate ourselves out of existence, if every blade of grass is mutated out of all recognition, life will go on in some form. How can anyone say it would be lower, worse, simply because it was different?'

'Well, let it be when I'm dead—'

'You will be, poor sweet,' said Tubby.

'—because as far as I'm concerned a world without humans is pointless.'

'What were men, *where* were men, a few million years ago?' Tom said.

'Why should I think in eons when my life span's so short?'

'You're a typical humanist, Agnes,' said Tubby, 'arrogant and out of date. Take a few biology lessons, humble yourself.'

'You should write up your defence of refineries for the Avon house magazine,' Hedley said quickly. 'I'm sure they'd like to be reassured.'

'They're always defending themselves,' Tom said, unaware of irony. 'Every issue carries something on fertilizers and pesticides. Oh yes, Avon permeates society with its benefactions. They claim they can make the desert flower. Spray dry soil with an emulsion mulch derived from their oil and it holds in what moisture there is long enough for the seed to germinate. Then you carry on with watering and irrigation.'

'My Petal Dew moisture cream works on the same principle,' I observed. 'Avon cosmetics!'

'I don't imagine they waste research on anything so frivolous,' said Helen.

'Not if it pays?'

But she had turned aside to talk to Hedley.

Why had I arranged it, why had I tried to be good, to do my duty? What was my reward? To hear Tom demonstrate in public the rift between my mind and his, to make Tubby cross enough to snub me, to see Hedley in his donkey coat smile and talk to Helen. The sooner I got back to Mittens the better.

We returned by the rough track of which one branch leads to the slant road and the other straight to Gunfleet.

'Isn't that Lenny, by the creek?' said Hedley.

'Yes, with his father. I expect they've been fishing.'

'For what?'

'Eels,' said Tubby, 'silver eels from the Atlantic. They feed in the Sargasso sea. All that way just to be caught by Lenny. Or rather by his father. Lenny couldn't catch a lame crab, poor chap, let alone an eel. As long as he doesn't fall in. There's a hell of a current.'

The grey water rippled among the reeds, where a single swan floated. But as we walked further from the river such illusions of freshness were left behind. The marsh became the dumping ground of industry, a waste of tips and smouldering fires, littered with worn rubber beltings and squares of canvas with ropes gymnasium thick at each corner, flung out, useless, finished, left to moulder, split and rot. Beside the path lay a ditch, a green scum of duckweed half hidden in a shoulder-high tunnel of dead fennel, its moss-choked sluices oozing not water but slime.

I was glad to get back to the street, dull and shuttered as it looked in the grey light, petrified in its mid-week silence; a fossil from the age of sail, when the Trade Winds mattered; a street, a whole village, in which no one had built a house since late in the reign of Victoria.

Hedley came and walked beside me. 'Life will go on,' he said, looking at the derelict cottage next to Woodey's; its silted roof was embossed with knobs of moss, the ridge matted with ragwort. 'Chalk dust and rain, that's all it needs.' He shot me one of his practised looks. 'Do you know why Tom was preferred to the geography department? The professor is known for tactless jeremiads on industrial monoliths.

His politics too. Pale blush rose. Enough to alarm Avon's security.'

'Walter told you this, I suppose. How did you come to know him so well?'

'We met in the army. We were seasick together, absolute equals.'

He seemed about to say more; but we had turned into the chalk-pit and I ran ahead to the cottage.

I'd spent most of the day shifting furniture to hide marks on the walls which Tom was too busy to decorate and I on principle left, hoping that when they got too bad we should have to move; then I had to shift cushions to hide the worn patches on the furniture. In spite of my efforts the room still looked untidy, littered with books, journals, records, the temporizers, the opiates with which we simultaneously drugged ourselves and wasted our substance.

Dearest docile Mittens, he was socially indispensable, something to admire and discuss as he scrambled and clung to Hedley. An animal, food, and drink; it was enough to keep us civil. And if Hedley was nice to Helen, that saved me the effort and the hypocrisy. He expressed sympathy for Ian's headache with what seemed genuine concern.

'Well of course I think sleeping tablets cause it,' she said. 'He said the headaches came from lack of sleep, but now they're worse than ever.'

'Perhaps he should wear glasses all the time,' I said. 'I get headaches when I need them changed—' I stopped. She merely shot me a glance that said *Who asked your advice?* And Hedley appeared not to have heard me.

Who mentioned algae? Tubby, I think, some time later. Hedley turned to Tom. 'I've never seen those slides. Would you show them to me?'

Tom went red. 'I would, with pleasure, but I haven't got my microscope.'

Tubby looked at his watch in an obvious way; as if we hadn't a clock.

'Have you lent it to Ian?' I said.

'No. Well, as a matter of fact, I've sold it.'

'What!'

'It was rather an extravagance,' he said, embarrassed.

Hedley's blue eyes met mine, steady, expressionless.

'I really must go,' Tubby said, rising with energy. 'Helen, shall we walk down together?'

She stood. Hedley put down the cat, and I picked it up. I was so bewildered that I hardly knew what to do.

'I think I'll take Mittens for a walk.'

'My dear Agnes, that euphemism is surely not applied to pussies?'

'I don't speak euphemisms. He often comes for a walk with me. They need exercise.'

'I can't think why you don't let the animal run about,' said Helen.

'He's too young. I'm afraid of the street, or a fox.'

'All that fuss. It's only a cat.'

'That's precisely what he's not,' Tubby said. 'He's an elegant Abyssinian aristocrat, slightly marred in the tail, but of pure untainted stock.'

His birth and breeding must cover his mistress, I thought. Hedley stood up quickly, sending Tubby a look I should have hated to receive. As if it mattered.

Mittens had been playing with his leash, and by the time I'd found it under the cooker they had all gone. Tom was clearing away the cups and plates.

'Leave them,' I said. 'I'll do it when I come in.' I hesitated.

There was so much we couldn't say to each other. Yet I couldn't ignore such a startling crack in my habit-hardened pattern of life. 'Why have you sold the microscope?' I asked. 'Why are you so hard up?'

'Oh—things mount up, you know.'

'I'll sell the car.'

'No, no. That's yours. There's no reason why you should—anyway, the test's so near it would be foolish to get rid of it now.'

He stroked Mittens' head. He was not particularly fond of cats, he did it to please me, to show that my effort with the salt pans hadn't gone unnoticed.

Why did he have to be so irreproachable? Why not boorish, cruel, drunk? Anything to deserve not being loved.

He carried the tray into the kitchen. I put my face against the cat's soft fur. Mittens, Mittens, I thought, what can I do? What ever can I do?

Nothing. Absolutely nothing.

The driving lessons went on, of course. I couldn't drop them for no given or apparent reason. Besides, it was too late for panic measures; the damage was done. The affair would have to run its course. Not to see him would only prolong it. Absence makes the heart grow fonder.

So we went one afternoon into the back country, a dry region of small farms and market gardens, a landscape of corn, cabbages, and pylons.

'The estuary casts a wide blight,' I said. 'Ten miles' depth each side of the river. After that it gets better—woods, valleys, streams, chalk downs. Roman country. Trust them to pick the best.'

'Tom lectured on Romans in the estuary.'

'Only the soldiers, poor mugs. No one built a villa on the marsh. It was vile then, as now.'

I went to change down at a road junction and did something I hadn't done in weeks, stuck the gear lever between third and second. He put his hand over mine and moved it down. What disruption! I forgot to look in the mirror, to signal, to look right as we turned. Yet there are people among whom such touches are small change.

'Why did you go to live in Gunfleet?' he said. 'I suppose I should say, why did Tom?'

I hesitated, selecting my words. 'Well, he knew from Ian that the cottage had fallen vacant. Ancrum's own that chalk-pit now, they've been meaning for years to put oil tanks in it. In the meantime they let the cottage to anyone who wants it. If not it would rot, it's no use to them. We were going to be there a couple of years, then move. Only—you know, things go on. We never seem to be able to hold on to money. Tom doesn't want me to work, and he doesn't want to give evening classes because that would take time from the museum and the marsh. Work means more to him than money.'

'Yet he's sold his microscope.'

'He used it less than Tubby.'

'You're still not selling the car?'

'I offered. He said the test is too close.'

'Yes it is,' he said thoughtfully. 'Try to remember to look in the mirror sometimes. Just make a gesture.'

'Can *you* understand what keeps those three men in such a dump?' I said after a minute. 'They're not brilliant, but they're able. Millions wouldn't even understand their general vocabulary, let alone some of the things they discuss. Why do they stay?'

'They work there.'

'At least they could move from Gunfleet.'

'It has a certain charm.'

'You should see it in a wet winter dusk. The end of the world.' I paused. 'There have been times when we could have gone. It isn't just money that's lacking, with Tom, it's the will. The same with all of them. People manage to do things if they really want to.'

'They've fallen in love with the marsh,' he said.

'But why?'

He shrugged. 'Why do people, adults, become all-absorbed in a hobby?'

I pulled up by the gate of the field. 'Well, tell me.'

He stubbed out his cigarette. 'Perhaps they've taken a look round and retired hurt.'

'Look at what?'

He shrugged. 'This whole lot, life in general. Or perhaps something's failed them, disappointed them, in themselves or outside.' He took out a new cigarette and lit it. 'Then of course, *cherchez la femme?*'

'What do you mean?'

'*Femme* means wife as well as woman.'

'Thanks,' I said. 'I suppose they fell in love with the marsh as they fell out with us, seeking consolation for their disappointment, their colossal irrevocable mistake.'

He smiled slightly. 'Ask yourself.'

'Well, in order of age, there's Tubby. Carole's slap-dashery would drive anyone to despair. Then Ian.' I had to force myself to speak with moderation, thinking of Helen. 'He buries himself in the marsh because he daren't raise his eyes to the things he'd like but can't afford. Or isn't allowed to afford.' I paused. 'Then there's Tom.'

'Go on,' he said. '*Cherchez la femme. La femme* who married him on the rebound, who only washes up once a day, who blew her savings on a superfluous car, who never counts the cost of Petal Dew and hand cream, who has the best clothes in Gunfleet and possibly in Shayle and Culham too—enough?'

'Listen, people talk about my extravagance. What about Carole's? Pink suède coats worn till they're solid with grease, hand-blocked wallpaper scribbled out of sight, animals with broken tails and kids with sore lips—'

'Tom has no children.'

'Because he doesn't want any.'

He raised his eyebrows. 'Life must go on.'

'He's confident it will, without his help.'

'Wouldn't *you* like something to take your mind off Gunfleet?'

'If you didn't know who or what your parents had been, would you rush to perpetuate the strain?'

'You're a pessimist. All you can say with certainty is that your father was wilful and your mother warm-hearted. Besides, you haven't tried very hard to find out, have you?' He smiled. 'People manage to do things if they really want to.'

I rubbed the windscreen clear of small insects.

'Your mother came from the north all the way to Shayle,' he went on. 'That suggests a connexion. On the other hand it may have been random, somewhere away from everyone she knew. Didn't you even know the solicitors who dealt with the money?'

To deny that would be too obvious a lie. 'Stenlock, in Culham,' I said.

'Of course they could have handled it from anywhere.' He frowned as if it troubled him.

I reached for the key. 'Shall we go on?'

He looked at me quickly. 'I've grown so used to saying what I like to you. You've given up trying to check me with aspersions on my eating habits. I'm sorry.'

'It's all right. I often think of it. Perforce.' I sat holding the key. 'My unfortunate mother. The squint must have been the last straw. After all, she can't have meant to have me.'

I was one of the thousands unthought of, unintended, the accidents, the surprises, received with dismay but finally accepted with a shrug, the luck of the game, the reluctant payment of ephemeral pleasures.

'I didn't mean to put you in this frame of mind,' he said.

'It's a frame of mind I have. You didn't make it.' I switched on the engine. 'Go on saying what you like. It's good for me. Besides, I started it this time, asking about the men.'

'Ah yes, the men,' he said. We moved out of the patch by the gate, into the road. 'Do you think this sticking to Gunfleet is entirely voluntary? Perhaps they'd like promotion, change.'

'They'd have got it. They're very good at their work.'

'That's not everything.' He hesitated. 'I think—this is cool to come from me—I think they're irresponsible.'

Schoolboys. It was what I often thought. 'But they have tremendous responsibility at work,' I said.

'I meant personally irresponsible. That may come out when their characters are assessed.'

'Only a few minutes ago they were three suffering martyrs.'

'You must have everyone black or white. Don't you understand? You can peel back causes and blame to infinity. You can say *cherchez le mari*, as well as *cherchez la femme*. They are martyrs, if you insist on so strong a word. But at the same time, Tubby begets four children and neglects them, that's to say leaves them entirely to Carole. Tom sets up house and neglects it—' He stopped.

'You can't say Ian's irresponsible or neglectful.'

'Why not?'

'Because he isn't,' I said hotly.

He used the dual control pedals to bring the car to a stop, pulled up the brake, and flicked the gear into neutral. The blue eyes turned on me, cool, steady, inscrutable.

'What are you looking at?' I asked, nervously.

'Heredity.'

I sat still for a moment. Then my heart began to thud with alarm. Not very steadily I put the gear into first. We were facing uphill; and the start I made was far from creditable. I drove on slowly and in silence.

When we came in sight of Sankton's he told me to pull in.

'What for?'

'Petrol.'

'Do we have to?'

'Look at the gauge.'

'I mean, must it be here?'

'Go on,' he said, with a sudden grin. 'I'll look after you.'

For some time there had been a new girl at the pumps, dark and bright-eyed, with quite a nice figure; but even the memory of Livia's melting radiance made her seem coarse. Sankton was lurking in the background, treating me to his infuriating pretence of respect. I caught the glances that flashed between him and Hedley by way of the girl; in which as plain as day Hedley deplored the change for the worse, and Sankton apologetically suggested it was the best they could do. Men! They were all brothers under the skin. It was a pleasure to see Lenny shambling along the road. I waved, and he lolloped over to me, beaming.

'Nice!' he said, touching the car.

'Would you like a ride?'

If he'd had a tail he'd have wagged it. I got out of the driving seat and into the back. Hedley moved to the wheel. Lenny, almost bursting with joy, sat down beside him. Sankton himself came to give me the change. The creature had the temerity to squeeze it into my hand.

I gave Hedley's shoulder a tap, in my annoyance rather a prod. 'Go on,' I said, 'we're ready.'

'Very good, my lady,' he said like a shot. Naturally Sankton was convulsed.

He drove forward slowly. And from behind the garage walked the green-eyed man I'd seen there weeks ago, on the Sunday when Hedley spoke to Livia, the animal man who had glared out of the shed, the Avon rogue who had stood beside Tom in the queue at Culham. We passed him, and turned into the drive.

Hedley had the tact to take the path. Lenny was gobbling incomprehensible comments, turning round every other moment to grin at me, waving regally as we passed some children. We reached the garage, or rather the two tumble-down sheds between the caravan and the cottage, in which we kept the cars and an ancient bicycle of mine.

Lenny lumbered out. Clumsy red giant! Hedley, so spare and grey, looked quite a waif beside him. 'Thank you very much,' he gobbled. For a moment I thought he was going to give us each a stone, since his hands were in his pockets, but with a final beam he jogged off; the way we'd just come, poor Lenny. By the caravan he stopped and pointed. 'Pussy,' he called, and ran on, turning across the chalk-pit to take the children's short cut through the bushes to the slant road.

I left Hedley to lock the car and ran up the path. The kitten was lying like a sphinx on the step of the caravan, its yellow eyes blinking at me, bland and mild. I picked him up. 'How did you get out, you wicked darling love?' I kissed him.

Hedley came up.

'Substitution,' he said dryly. He opened the door, and like a flash Mittens leapt out of my arms and ran inside. I went to go after him, and hesitated.

'Go in,' he said. 'It's your caravan.'

Mittens was sitting on the bunk. I picked him up, glancing round quickly. Apart from the books and papers on the table it was quite tidy. He had a couple of cooking pans that he'd bought for himself, since we needed ours at the cottage.

'I hope you eat properly,' I said.

'Enough.' He opened the window. 'Did you see the Avon pilferer at Sankton's?'

'Yes. Birds of a feather, I suppose.' There was a photograph in a folding frame on the shelf; I was trying unobtrusively to look at it.

'What have you got against Sankton?' he said. 'More than his generally suspect character, isn't it?'

'If I tell you you'll be the only person who knows. Apart from Sankton himself.'

'Go on. I'll be honoured.'

I had to laugh. 'You won't, when you know. It was just a ludicrous incident some years back, before he took over the garage. I was still working in Mediham. One afternoon coming home I got in an empty carriage and he followed me, sat down opposite, a stranger then, of course. After a few minutes he caught my eye—not exactly a wink. A gleam, a suggestion. I'm sure you know what I mean. I can't understand to this day what took his fancy. There was I with glasses, red pencil, piles of marking—'

'What were you wearing? That pink dress?'

'Don't be silly. This was three years ago.' I stared at the photograph on the shelf; but the light was shining on its mica.

'Well?' he said. 'Is that all? You carry on a vendetta against him for having dared to give you one look?'

'I don't have any vendetta,' I said. 'When we were coming to Culham I saw he was getting ready to go. He sat right forward on the edge of the seat, his knees were nearly touching mine. I remembered the line runs under the chalk into the station, and I'd just thought *that's when he'll*—and we went in the tunnel. He stroked my knee, so gently, I was amazed, just brushed it with his fingers. It's only a short tunnel, straight to the platforms, and he stood up. I said to him "Did I ask for any attentions from you?" Do you know, he leaned down to me with such a smile, and he said "No, but you deserve them." Then he got out. So should I have done, but I stayed on till Shayle.' I paused. 'A little while later I saw him at the garage. He smiled, just once. Since then he's treated me like a princess, the hypocrite.'

'Never said anything?'

'Not a word.'

He nodded. 'He let you off lightly, if you consider what he might have attempted between Mediham and Culham. It's quite a long run. He knew just how far he could go without running into trouble.'

'I'm sure he's a skilled worker.'

'And an accomplished one. You didn't dislike what he did.'

'Well, it wasn't on the same level as the average crude pass from a strange man, which is just disgusting, if they only knew it. He was so delicate, there was no offence in it, I couldn't be cross.'

'That's the trouble, isn't it?' he said. 'You make him keep his distance not because you're outraged but because you *weren't* and you're afraid you wouldn't be if he tried it again. He's a true Don Juan. Opportunism, effrontery, divination, and charm. Irresistible, it seems.'

Why should he say it with envy? I turned to the table, which was covered with textbooks and written papers crossed with red ink. 'Is this your Russian? Who marks it?'

'I do. I keep going back till I've got it right.' Suddenly he reached across and put the photograph on the table in front of me.

'Sorry,' I said, blushing. All the same I looked, since he'd offered. The image was slightly blurred, as if it had been too much enlarged or perhaps taken with a telescopic lens, I don't understand these things: a woman in a light belted raincoat, looking not directly at the camera, but up and out, rather anxiously, as if she were waiting for a bus. Perhaps I thought that because I could see the edges of other people beside her, and a smudged face behind. *Don't ask questions.* But he'd thrust it at me. 'Who is it?'

He put the photograph back without looking at it. 'Someone who said no.'

To him! She was just ordinary. She had nice eyes and very fair hair.

'I'm sorry,' I said.

'So am I.' He leaned against the door. 'I told you I'm sentimental. My heart's been broken so many times it's getting beyond it.'

'So you think a heart can break more than once.'

'Yes. It'll mend in time, like a limb. And like a limb it's never quite what it was.'

We seemed to have nothing more to say. He smiled briefly, and stood back to let me pass. I departed, clinging to the cat.

He pined for that blonde heartbreak. I was wasting my time, and making a fool of myself into the bargain. Running after him. Yet he didn't have to give me lessons, he didn't have to come and live in our caravan; above all he didn't have to speak to me that first time, months back, that evening in The Ship when I was waiting alone for the men, wearing the pink dress, playing with the solitaire board. Why did he do it? What did he expect?

I unlocked the kitchen door. For three years a generous country had invested in me, kept me at Harefield mulling over the accumulated wisdom of five centuries in the mother tongue alone. I was not a whit the better, wiser, or happier. My knowledge hadn't saved me, and couldn't console.

I dropped the car key in the table drawer. I always kept it there, together with my house purse. Tom, Ian, Tubby, and Hedley had each in turn told me how rash this was. But it saved the bother and probable mishaps of transferring from one handbag to another. Even in Gunfleet I wouldn't carry a handbag that didn't suit what I was wearing. Agnes's vanity, Agnes's extravagance. They didn't know. Appearance was the discipline that kept me going.

I went upstairs and brushed my well-cut mouse-brown hair. I opened the wardrobe and pulled from the back the dress I'd been wearing that afternoon three years before, when I'd met Sankton on the train. It was faded, but I could still wear it.

Chapter Eight

THE DAY WE WENT ON THE PICNIC—

Agnes, wake up! *Wake up.* It was yesterday. Only yesterday. Sunday, twenty-eight hours ago, when our cracked and loosened foundations finally parted, launching us on a landslide, gently, imperceptibly, on the hill yesterday afternoon, when we stopped in the lane, behind the Jag and the firecracker pulled on the grass by a gate in the hedge. I remembered the silence as Tom switched off the engine, the close warmth of the wooded bank that reached me as I got out, the slam of the door, the sound of two rising larks as we climbed over the padlocked gate to join the others in the field.

Tubby's boys were rolling in some half-hearted scrap. Sorrel was being swung at arm's length by Carole's father. Malcolm and Hedley were playing with a ball. Tansy, crying in quiet hopelessness, hung on the back of Carole's skirt. Her grandmother had retreated behind dark glasses and the shade of a vast straw hat. A cigarette stuck out of her wide red mouth. She looked like a totem pole.

Carole was midstream in complaint as we arrived.

'Isn't this too bad of them?' she cried to Helen. 'Didn't we definitely agree to go to Boxford?'

'My dear, I've already explained,' Tubby put in wearily while Helen was still drawing breath. 'Ian and Tom and I settled a long while back to come and see the *Hordelymus* today. If you *will* arrange these outings the night before—'

'But we've always done it impromptu, you know we have, that's half the fun. I really don't see that an afternoon out with tea and a few sandwiches calls for long notice. Agnes, didn't you say it would be all right with you? Did you know they'd planned to see this wretched plant, whatever it is?'

I hated being appealed to, but I had to support her. Tom hadn't told me, it really was his fault.

Helen turned to Ian.

'What I fail to understand is why you said nothing when I told you we'd arranged it.'

He looked uncomfortable. 'Well we thought we could get this done first, then go on to Boxford.'

'But we've come in exactly the opposite direction. It would take over an hour to get there now.'

'Why not stay here?' said Tubby. 'Nice view, plenty of grass. The kids can pick blackberries.'

'But we chose Boxford specially for the river and the swings.'

'Anyway I'm sure this is private,' said Helen. 'That gate wouldn't be chained and padlocked if we were meant to go through.'

Tubby merely turned aside with a shrug.

'It's all very well,' said Carole, aggrieved. 'You're not proposing to keep the children amused. You have enough time for your plants and birds, surely, without spoiling their treat.'

Treat! I doubted if it were that, even for the children. The rest of us endured Carole's sudden schemes, invariably broached at a time of maximum inconvenience, as an evil slightly less than the plaintive offence that refusal would have caused.

Tubby looked round. There was a momentary lull in the fights and games with which the children had passed the time. We were grouped together as if awaiting decision on the next move. Tubby wiped his hand over his forehead. 'Hot, isn't it?' he said. 'I could sink half a ton of ice cream.'

What could have possessed him! The words were hardly out of his mouth when his three eldest children began to vociferate for ices. Nothing would silence them, no appeals, no promises, not even the final invitation from Tubby to look round and tell him where the ice cream was to come from.

'If we'd gone to Boxford they could have bought ices in the sweet shop,' Carole said, oozing injury and reproach.

Then they started clamouring to go to Boxford. Finally their grandfather, either in indulgence or to save himself further nervous torture, offered to drive them in the Jag to the nearest village. Tansy started to howl at the idea of being left behind, so she was bundled in too. Then Carole in a fit of mother love decided that she couldn't let them scramble about the back of the car alone.

'Can I have an ice?' said Malcolm.

'Certainly not,' Helen said promptly. 'You've been twice to the dentist this holiday.'

For a second he looked as if he were going to appeal to his father; but Ian turned away.

With ill-concealed satisfaction Tubby watched the Jag move off. 'Right,' he said. 'We'll just slip in the wood while they're gone.'

Tom and Ian were already making for the trees at the side of the field. I started to walk with Tubby.

'You don't want to come, my dear Agnes,' he said hurriedly, 'you won't be interested. It's only a grass, a barley, nothing to look at.'

'If that's all couldn't it have waited?' said Helen.

Tubby chose not to hear.

'I hope they know where to look for it,' Hedley said. 'That's quite a big wood.'

Its full extent was hidden from us by the curve of the slope. We were about twenty-two miles from the river, folded in secretive Roman hills.

Hedley turned to Malcolm.

'Shall we see if we can find some blackberries in the hedge?'

'Don't let him eat any,' said Helen, 'the pips will ruin his teeth. I suppose *we* must await everyone's pleasure.'

She sent a glance of stony disapproval at Carole's mother, whose shoulders and back, though she was nearly sixty, were smooth, bronzed, and liberally exposed by her sun-top dress. Helen was wearing some hideous bargain cotton.

The blackberries on the hedge were poor and hardly ripe except for a few at the top that even Hedley couldn't reach. I ruined fifteen shillings-worth of stocking. After a time we gave up and played ball; but it was hot, and Malcolm easily tired. So we sat down by the two women. I tucked my legs under my skirt so that the laddered stocking should escape Helen's notice. She wouldn't fail to ask what I'd paid for them.

Hedley had taken out a pencil and pocket book, and was amusing Malcolm with some game. They might have been father and son. Hedley, Hedley! I couldn't escape him.

He'd been called in because Carole's parents had contrived to damage their car, causing a last minute transport shortage that would have persuaded anyone but Carole to drop the scheme. Helen had suggested that she drive my car; but since it had been cleaned and serviced ready for the test I refused, thereby vastly increasing her love for me.

The sun beat down, drawing a sweetish smell from the blackberry hedge, which attracted swarms of flies. The grass on which we sat was prickly with thistles.

'I'm hot,' said Malcolm. 'Can't we go in the wood and look for Dad?'

'All right,' Hedley said, standing up. He held out his hand to me. 'Will you come, Agnes?'

I was glad enough to leave Helen and Carole's mother to stew in mutual scorn.

Beyond its stinging nettle fringe the wood was quite pleasant, crossed by grass rides that made walking easy. When we'd gone some way Malcolm found a colony of early toadstools pushing through the grass at the edge of the path.

'Are they poisonous?' he asked, nervously fascinated.

'I don't know,' said Hedley, 'so don't touch them.'

I broke one of the stems with my foot. The underside of the cap was sulphur yellow, smooth, punctured with hundreds of tiny holes like sponge rubber. 'It's a boletus,' I said, glad enough to appropriate the crumbs that fell from Tom's table. 'Some of them are poisonous.'

Hedley picked up a stick and prodded the sponge. A blue-green bruise appeared at once where he'd crushed it.

Malcolm started back with a gesture of revulsion. 'It's bleeding.'

'No it isn't,' I said quickly, 'that's just a stain. Listen, there's a woodpecker.' I hadn't heard a thing, but it distracted his attention. Hedley rather guiltily dropped the stick. 'There it is again,' I lied. 'Over there.' I pointed away from the toadstools. And thus I saw Tubby.

He was walking through the wood, very slowly, very quietly, almost stealing along, looking about him all the time. He hadn't seen us, I suppose, because we were standing so still among the trees waiting for the drill of the non-existent woodpecker. Whatever Tubby was looking for, it was not *Hordelymus europaea.* That was not the botanist's creep, with head lowered and eyes fixed to the ground.

I stepped from behind the tree. 'Hullo Tubby,' I called. 'Any luck?'

How he jumped! But he came across to us quickly enough. 'No go,' he said, 'not a blade. The place is too big.'

'Where are the others?'

'We split up. They're about.' He gave a piercing whistle. 'Shall we wend our way to the tea flasks? Thirsty work, this plunging about woods.'

'Aren't you going to wait for Tom and Ian?'

'They'll make their own way back when they're ready. They heard me whistle.'

I didn't see how he could be sure. However, they were not babies. Only schoolboys. We turned back along the ride, and Malcolm informed Tubby that we had heard a woodpecker; such is the power of suggestion.

'Agnes heard it,' Hedley corrected him. 'Or said she did.'

'I dare say,' said Tubby, 'they're quite common.'

'What are those little birds at the top of that oak?' Hedley said suddenly.

Tubby stared. 'Warblers of some kind.' His hand groped for his binoculars and met nothing. He looked down, taken aback for a second.

'Left them in the car?' I said.

'No, I think they're at home.'

For Tubby to come out without his binoculars was unheard of. But Malcolm was running ahead.

We came into the open just as the Jag reappeared. Through its sun roof rose the head and shoulders of Chervil, the eldest boy, who was standing on the front seat; the remains of a pink ice were smeared on the roof of the car. In spite of his professed thirst Tubby immediately exerted himself to amuse the sticky brood. The next quarter of an hour was spent in wild games of touch and rolling the children down the slope, while Carole enlarged on their search for a village and a sweet shop. But when Ian and Tom came out of the wood together Tubby abruptly abandoned his children. His face was scarlet, running with sweat; he must have lost several ounces on that hill.

Tea passed as it usually did on our outings. Carole's children smeared their chops with jam and inadvertently squirted orange juice in each other's eyes. Malcolm and Ian forced down hard-boiled egg and practically dry bread.

'You didn't find your grass, then?' Hedley said to Ian.

'No. There probably isn't much of it. We'd need more time.'

'Suppose you had found it, what would you have done? Picked a bit for pressing? Or taken a photograph?' He looked at Ian. 'Did you bring your camera?'

'No.' Ian turned to Helen. 'Is there any tea left in the flask?'

'I'm hot,' said Malcolm. He looked rather pale.

'You shouldn't have run about so much,' said his sympathetic mother. Tubby looked foolish. His father-in-law passed over a newspaper, which had been picked up with the picnic basket from the boot of the Jag, for Malcolm to use as a fan.

'Why don't you make a paper hat?' Hedley suggested.

Then they all wanted paper hats, even Tansy. Hedley was turned into a machine which it was my task to feed with sheets of raw material. I skipped with interest through gossip and pictures. It was the kind of paper which entered the cottage only as wrapping. Alas. On the front page a small headline caught my eye. *Refinery Wage Grab.* Masked bandits yesterday made off with over £2,000 from a van carrying wages to men employed on a new laboratory at the Avon refinery, Shayle. The driver of the van—

I glanced at the date. It was only yesterday's paper. 'There's been a wage robbery at Avon, Tom, did you know?'

'Yes, it was in the paper.'

I read the rest of the short paragraph. Yesterday had been one of Tom's Saturdays on duty at the museum. He always took the paper with him to work, I never saw it till the evening; and yesterday evening I'd tried to make inroads on a mounting pile of ironing. 'You didn't mention it,' I said.

He shrugged. 'It's not very spectacular. They didn't get much, and the chaps in the van were only stunned.'

Hedley held out his hand for the sheet.

'Poor Walter,' I said, 'he'll have his security men on the carpet.'

'It wasn't directly Avon money,' said Tom. 'An outside contractor's doing the building.'

A short discussion ensued between Helen, Carole, and her parents, on wage robberies in general. Helen advocated payment by cheque, Carole's father the weekly changing of vehicle and guards and varying of time and route.

'There's not much you can do about the end of the route,'

Hedley said. He'd been reading the paragraph, I noticed, as he made Chervil's hat. 'If you're taking wages to the refinery you have to arrive sometime. These were attacked in the road leading to the gates. Besides, you'll never be able to rule out inside leaks.'

The children, bored with adult inattention, began to fret for more games. Carole insisted that they end their tea with a piece of bread and butter.

'What do you think?' Tubby said quietly to Tom and Ian. 'Shall we go on to Boxford?'

'It will take too long,' said Ian. 'I don't want to be late home.'

Tubby nodded. 'We'll move off soon, then. Just give them a bit longer to play about.'

Chervil and Fennel immediately started badgering to go in the wood.

'It's very thick,' said Tom. 'I think you'd get lost.'

Such caution was greeted with outcry.

'Look, I'll tell you what,' Tubby said hastily, 'we'll have a quick game of hide and seek. Hiding in twos, not further than ten yards from the edge. Only two minutes start to get hidden and three grown-ups to be seekers.'

This task he allotted to himself, his father-in-law, and Hedley. The rest paired up, long-suffering in the cause of humouring the kids. Sorrel, whose tender years at present camouflaged her flagrant chasing, made a beeline for Ian; Carole kept Tansy, Helen seized the unfortunate Malcolm, Tom went with Chervil.

'It's all right,' I said, 'I'll hide on my own.'

I don't know how the others concealed themselves. I simply ploughed into the bracken and knelt down. It was like being in the sea, an even level of translucent green filtered with sunlight, still and cool. In what seemed far less than two minutes Tubby's warning whistle sounded. I heard twigs cracking to my left and raised my head to the top of the fronds. Someone moved in the bushes. I looked the other way, in time to see Hedley's back as he ran straight down the ride along which we'd walked with Malcolm.

I couldn't think why he should hare so purposefully towards the heart of the wood; unless he hadn't heard the embargo on deep hiding. I hesitated, stood up, pushed through the bracken, ripping my undamaged stocking on a bramble, and went after him.

He could run, with his long legs; but so could I. By the patch of boletus with its single broken plant I caught sight of him; then a stone slipped in my shoe and I stopped to shake it out. He disappeared round a turn of the path. I didn't want to call out in case the others heard. I ran on again, till the bend brought me suddenly to a small clearing from which a ride lay at right angles to the one by which we'd come. It was the end of the wood. A flint wall about seven feet high extended left and right. A door was let into it; and by this he stood with his back to me.

'Hedley,' I said.

His head lifted slightly but he didn't turn. 'I shan't be a minute,' he said calmly.

I leaned against a tree, realizing and blushing for my own stupidity. In a few moments he came up to me.

'What is it?' he said. 'Anything wrong?'

'I'm sorry, I saw you running up the path. I thought you didn't know we were going to hide near the edge.'

He smiled slightly. 'Next time you see an adult making off in a wood, stop and ask yourself if they haven't a simple reason.'

Perhaps some biochemical reaction made me unreasonably angry; I had obscure notions of adrenalin released by the effort of running. 'Why did you come all this way? Why not go into the trees?'

'Can't I even choose my own place to—pass water?'

'Go on choosing public paths and you'll be run in.'

His eyes glinted at me. 'We're on private land.'

I couldn't think of an answer, but I refused to knuckle under. I walked across the clearing to the door in the wall. There was no handle, no keyhole. The wall was a kind quite common in the district, faced with large split flints, smooth and dark and close-set. The curved top bristled with flint flakes packed edge-on in concrete; they were like the primitive arrowheads in the case at the Shayle Museum, sharp as razors.

I turned to Hedley, who was watching me intently. 'I suppose it all belongs to the house on the corner.'

He didn't answer. I looked along the ride which ran parallel with the wall. I couldn't see to the end; but I noticed marks in the soft green ground. 'Tyre tracks,' I said. 'It must join the road.'

'Get away!'

'I told you it's a public path,' I retorted.

A dog barked somewhere beyond the wall; a deep heavy bark, almost a bay.

'You hear?' he said. 'We're trespassing. Let's go.'

'Coward.'

The dog barked again, closer. We walked together out of the clearing and back along the ride.

At the edge of the field we came face to face with Tubby. 'Haven't you found anyone?' I asked.

'Everyone, my dear Agnes, except *you*.' He looked sharply from me to Hedley. 'We were thinking of going.'

But Fennel and Chervil had seized the moment when everyone's back was turned to slip into the wood. It took all five men nearly ten minutes to catch them, the prize being shared by Carole's father and Hedley. Tansy was fratchy with fatigue, Sorrel and the boys were overexcited. Tom looked gloomy, and Ian's forehead was so knotted that I was sure he had a headache. It was a typical ending to one of Carole's excursions; only she could weather them more or less unchanged.

'Agnes, come with us this time,' said Malcolm, dragging me towards Hedley's car.

I hesitated by Tom. 'Do you mind?'

'No, no,' he said absently, 'just as you like.'

'Malcolm,' Helen called, 'I want to find you ready for bed when I get home.'

There was not room to turn in the road. We went half a mile before coming to an open gate into which Hedley could reverse. A few minutes later we passed the Jag, then Tom, still by the hedge, then the gated entrance to the green ride by the wall, which continued for a couple of hundred yards to the end of the lane.

I couldn't see the house, secluded in its wooded grounds. It was far enough from the river once to have been the home of the rich; but even here they no longer lived. Their large houses had become their utilities: schools, golf clubs, hotels, clinics.

As we nosed forward at the crossroads a large car turned out of the gates to our left. Another was pulled up at the lodge.

'They have cars to match their dogs,' I observed. 'I wonder what it is.'

'Still a private house, perhaps. Or some sort of country club.'

'Rather remote.'

He smiled. 'Maybe it's that sort of club.'

'What do you mean?'

'Well—licensing laws, you know, or gambling,' he said evasively.

Chervil leaned forward. 'When can we go fast?'

'When we're on the main road. Sit back or I'll stop and give you a good cuff.'

Chervil subsided. We hugged the banks of lanes that never seemed to pass through villages, only to wind towards them as the signposts pointed, Lawne, Datcham, Framley, and like a forlorn hope, an impossible distant mirage, Shayle, twenty-two.

'Luscious car,' said Malcolm. 'Roll on the main road. I love whizzing past all the people, specially if they're waiting for a bus.'

'You horror,' I said. But he was only voicing my secrets.

You're a despicable worm, Agnes, vain as they come, I thought. You love to be seen next to this dazzling masculine item, so that everyone thinks you're his wife, that your merits have won this glorious prize, even that you've borne him two handsome sons. False pretences. Borrowed plumes. He isn't yours, he's the blonde woman's. And you're not his, you're Tom's.

We couldn't go fast on the main road because of the traffic from the coast. It was full evening when we walked towards the boys' two homes, the warp-roofed rosy Georgian house and the small Victorian villa.

'Can we go on the swings?' said Chervil.

Hedley glanced at his watch. 'Three minutes.'

'They've had the best part of the day at the end,' I said as they rushed off. 'Perhaps it'll make up to Chervil for having to finish tea with bread and butter. Carole's nanny taught her it was the thing to do. Poor kids! Didn't you always save the jammiest bit of bread till last?'

'We had dripping mostly. You go for the brown bits. There was treacle sometimes.'

'When you were well off?'

He smiled at me, and I turned away. I didn't want him to be nice to me, I hadn't the strength to bear it.

Lenny was jogging along the concrete path towards us, accompanied by a fat child in a cotton dress, that same demi-trollop Marian whom Helen had rescued from the swing rope weeks before, and whom only a few days ago I had seen swinging in a semi-stupor from side to side of the hole. As they reached us Lenny stopped. Marian ran between the posts to the street.

'Hullo Lenny,' I said.

The beaming giant clenched his fist by his ear and emitted guttural sounds, pointing his other paw at Tubby's house.

'He means he heard the phone ringing,' said Malcolm: Hedley had whistled the boys off the swings dead on time.

'All right, Lenny, thanks. I'll tell him,' I said.

He ambled away, quietly repeating his telephone noise, which seemed to give him pleasure; perhaps he was proud of it.

'Come on, freckles, you've to get to bed,' said Hedley.

For one bewildering moment I thought he was talking to me. I'd forgotten the lavish sprinkling over Malcolm's little snub nose.

'Will you stay down here till they come?' he said to me. 'Promise? Don't go away.'

'I promise. I'll go round the back, you can see me out of your window.'

'You too.' He looked up at Hedley with his grey eyes and charming lifted smile, so like his father's.

'All right. Have you enjoyed yourself?'

'Yes, thank you. The only thing about picnics is the day after.'

Hedley raised his eyebrows, inviting me to notice this early cynicism.

'You know,' Malcolm went on, 'eating the crusts off the sandwiches for breakfast.'

Hedley went scarlet. I was too hardened, I who had been a teacher, recipient of a thousand intimate revelations. If parents only knew the secrets their innocent children betray!

We said good night, and walked round to the garden at the back.

'You're fond of him, aren't you?' said Hedley. 'That surprises me, considering that he's half Helen. How did they meet, his parents? In the army?'

'No, after, when Ian was a student. He went to London, not Harefield. He lodged in Helen's parents' house.' I paused. 'Perhaps her horrors hadn't developed, matured. Then whatever *you* say, in the accepted sense he's so conscientious. I suppose he thought marriage demanded solid virtues. And here was a healthy sensible thrifty person trained in domestic science—he was young, twenty-three. You can be sure she snatched the chance. She's four years older than him, you know.'

'And he's very handsome, even now.'

'Yes, he is,' I said quickly. 'Well her father said he didn't advise marriage till they had a home of their own and at least five hundred in the bank. You see where she gets it from. They were engaged five years.'

Malcolm appeared at his bedroom window. I waved.

'Long enough for him to change his mind,' Hedley observed.

'I dare say he did. It wouldn't make any difference. He'd said he'd marry her, he'd feel bound by his word, it would be his duty.'

'Duty! Don't you think it might have been fairer, honester, braver, to break it off? Where in hell does it come from, this sickening senseless ethic? You marry Tom, Ian marries Helen, because you think marriage ought to be safe, prudent, because you think you *ought,* not because you love them. No wonder Tom's driven to his marsh and she to her societies, her relentless heartless do-gooding. Aren't they the equivalents of Petal Dew, dresses, cars, dogs, hamsters, canaries? Time killers, life fillers.'

'Very clever,' I said. 'She may have been driven, but she revels in them now. Besides, it's her parsimony that I can't stand, the eternal eye on the bank balance, the joint account. I know you'll take her part, you're always nice to her.'

'I'm sorry for her.'

'What about Malcolm and Ian, chewing their way through the picnic crusts? Why don't you feel sorry for them?'

'I can leave that to you.'

The two cars came down the drive. I called good night to Malcolm and went out to the Promenade. I didn't want to speak to Ian and Helen; but they were with Tom, who had pulled up his car by the posts. Tubby was backing the Jag towards the garage.

Tom came across to me. 'Sorry we were so long. Tubby

stopped to ring his friend at Lindhurst. He says the nightjars have been churring the past couple of evenings at dusk. We thought we'd go to hear them.'

'Now?'

'Well yes, there's no knowing how long this churring's likely to go on.'

Such fits and starts had lost their power to surprise me. 'Why's Tubby putting the car away, then?'

'We'll go in mine, it's easier to manoeuvre along a farm lane. This wood's about a mile off the road.'

They were mad to go out again after the exhausting afternoon. Lindhurst was fifteen miles south of Culham. I looked at Ian. His forehead hadn't magically smoothed itself out, if anything it was worse. Perhaps he preferred driving about the countryside with a headache to reckoning with Helen's pent-up displeasure.

Tubby came down the drive, attempting nonchalance in the face of Carole's reproachful looks.

'Party of ornithologists up the road,' he informed us. 'Some London group coming to the marsh for the night flights.'

'Lenny heard your phone while we were out,' I said. 'Anything you've forgotten?'

'Not that I know, my charmer.'

For a second the controller of an able brain looked through his smooth waffler's mask, and I had an impression of indefinable tension between us. The moment passed, however, as with languid farewells the party drifted to its release.

Tubby made for Tom's car.

'What about your binoculars?' said Hedley.

'My dear chap, in the dark?'

Hedley turned to Ian. 'Couldn't you listen to this churring to get an idea of their position, then take a shot with a flash?'

Ian hesitated.

'Well if we don't buck up we shan't even hear the bloody birds, old man,' said Tubby.

Ian hurriedly thanked Hedley for bringing home Malcolm and got in the car. Tom drove along the street and turned to take the chalk-pit path to the top, swinging wide to avoid the wall at the end of the alley.

'You're getting very interested in wildlife,' I said to Hedley. 'You've taken the taint from them.'

He fished Chervil's paper hat from the small back seat of his car and put it absently in my hand. 'It's not the wildlife that interests me,' he said, 'it's the stripping of medals from the men.'

'What do you mean?'

'Perhaps the camera and binoculars have gone the way of Tom's microscope.'

I tried to remember when I had last seen Ian and Tubby with their toys, but I couldn't. I'd seen them so little, and with such indifference, since Hedley came.

'What does it matter, anyway,' I said wearily.

'Don't forget you've got your test tomorrow.'

'No. I'm going to wash my hair now.'

He smiled. 'It's the other mirror that counts.'

'Good night,' I said. 'Thanks for the ride.'

He reversed, and swung the car round the corner of the drive, taking it up to Sankton's to put it away. In the draught the newspaper hat fluttered from my hand. I picked it up and carried it to the litter bin by the bus stop, staring idly at the print. By the peak I could see our local excitement, the tiny paragraph, half folded. Four masked bandits. Refinery gates. A green Jowett Javelin ABL or ABF or ABE–

I shoved the hat in the bin. Good luck to you, mates, I thought crudely. They'll hook you for your paltry two thousand. You must chisel in millions before they'll let you get by.

I walked up the dusty street. The Sunday bikes were clustered in the kerb, the jukebox throbbed in The Ship. How long, what weeks, since we'd been inside! I glanced in the private bar. It was empty.

The evening quietly closed the weary day. I washed and set my hair. The sky was quite dark when I finished. Mittens and I had sat down together in the kitchen to have our supper of milk and biscuit when there was a knock at the door.

'Who is it?' I called.

'Hedley.'

I jumped up. 'Wait a minute.' I snatched the pins from the rollers and tore them out, feeling across my forehead the ominous soft flop of half-dried hair. I should look a mess in the morning. I opened the door.

'I'm sorry,' he said. 'Could you let me have some candles? I've left my torch in the car and my gas has run out. Either squirrels or children have pulled the tube off the container.'

'Come in,' I said. Mittens had already run to be picked up. I opened the cupboard and took out the tin box. 'You're not going to work by candlelight, I hope.' That would never do, to strain and blemish those pure candid blue eyes.

'Have you ever tried to get yourself to bed in absolute pitch blackness?' he said. 'I don't want to knock milk, water, and food over your caravan.'

'Mind you don't set fire to it.' I turned round. He was smiling away to himself. 'What's amusing you?' I asked.

'Your feminine vanity. You might as well have left your hair as it was. I'd seen you through the window.'

In my confusion I couldn't think of a good smart retort, but spoke at random. 'Tubby sometimes says I'm unfeminine.'

'Tubby says too much for his own good,' he said curtly. His face relaxed. 'You're feminine all right. Impulsive, frivolous, selfish, extravagant, vain.' He raised his well-practised eyebrow. 'What's the matter?'

'That hurt.'

'Because you know it's true. Anyway, it's my turn.'

'When have I ever hurt you?'

'Think what you've said about tripe.'

'I'm sorry. I'm terribly sorry, I didn't mean you to take it seriously.'

'I always take tripe seriously. I entertain very tender feelings for tripe.'

He was teasing me, playing with me. 'I detest being treated like a schoolgirl,' I said.

'You shouldn't act like one.'

I'd asked for it. And if Tom was a schoolboy we were aptly matched.

'Quite often you look like one,' he added.

I tried to push my hair out of my eyes.

'That's it,' he said, enjoying himself hugely. 'How did you know?'

'Obviously you haven't looked at schoolgirls' heads. Otherwise you'd know they all have sophisticated haircuts.'

'I do know,' he said unabashed. 'They wear their berets like skewered pancakes.'

'Asking for trouble.'

'What a dragon you must have been to your pupils. Do as I say, not as I do.' He looked at my hair. 'It isn't the cut, it's the texture and colour. That fine soft mouse.'

'I had it blonded once, a couple of years ago,' I said; and hoped my voice sounded normal to him.

He didn't comment. I gave him the candles.

'Have you ever heard a nightjar churring?' he asked.

'No, and I don't suppose *they* will. It's probably electricity cables humming. Give me the cat, or he'll follow you, and he's not to have his precious fur singed.'

'Good night, little substitute,' he said stroking Mittens' ears. 'Perhaps Tubby meant unnatural rather than unfeminine.'

'I'm quite natural. A natural child, in fact.'

'That's your excuse,' he said sharply. 'If everyone stopped to consider their ancestry the race would die out. Or should. Unreflecting generation may be vain, smug and thoughtless, but it keeps things turning.' He gave me the cat. 'Aren't you really afraid of losing your freedom, your easy life, your thousand small luxuries?'

'We were poor, I had to work.'

'You don't now.'

Now! It was too late now. He was so eager to chastise me, he remembered so much; couldn't he remember the flood wall? Poor Tom. He didn't deserve what had happened. But I didn't love him, I didn't want his children. And he didn't want mine. There was so much Hedley didn't know, with his almighty cleverness; and I couldn't tell him.

'Don't take it to heart, Agnes,' he said. 'I'm only talking to pass time, like Tubby. All right?'

I nodded. He gave Mittens a final pat, and went away, and I could shut the door.

Don't take it to heart. If only I could have laughed or reasoned or sneered myself out of it, if only I were one of the fortunate cynics to whom it's only a game, an ironical titter. Couldn't he understand, he who claimed to be sentimental? I was just a spineless feminine jelly, hurt by what he said, even more hurt to let him go. What had he done to reduce me to this depth? What did I know of him, apart from what I could see? What was he?

A man, I suppose. Not a puppy, not a schoolboy, a man. That was all. That was enough.

He wouldn't have found me so unnatural as he imagined.

Chapter Nine

IT WAS RAINING WHEN I FAILED THE TEST THIS MORNING, squalls slashing up the estuary, streaming over the windscreen, curdling like smoke on the roads. I sat in the car afterwards listening to the examiner politely explain my errors, encourage me to persevere; watching for Hedley in his black mac.

He came round the corner of Howe Street: perhaps he'd waited in the library. I thanked the examiner, we got out. I didn't wait. Hedley could move the car, take it back, do what he liked with it. I went down the short cut to Anson Place, past the traffic, the lights, and turned down the narrow cleft of the road to the ferry.

He came after me on his great long shanks, caught me easily as I dodged among the shoppers and seamen and blue-coated Lascars. Traffic from the ferry was creeping up the cobbled street, which was half choked by parked vans and cars. A lorry had mounted the pavement. He put his hand on my arm and drew me into the door of a shop.

'You hate to lose, don't you?' he said. 'You can't bear not to have conquered the examiner and the regulations.'

A gust caught the loose side blind of the shop, slapping it backwards and forwards like a sail.

'I wanted to get out,' I said.

'Altogether? Leave Tom?'

'No. At least—I don't know, I really don't know. Just to get in the car sometimes and drive away, out of this vile place, go somewhere beautiful, interesting, civilized, Bath, Edinburgh, even just up to London, anywhere at all to get out of here. You don't know the hours I spend dreaming of other places. You won't understand, you think Gunfleet has charm, because you know you can leave any time.'

The lorry edged by, hemming us in the doorway, blocking out everything but its blank grey side.

'Why do you have to have a car?' he said. 'There are trains.'

'But to get up and go when you want, without fuss, throw everything in the back, never think of timetables and luggage and tickets—'

'You'll pass in the end.'

'How can I keep the car when he's short of money? And once I sell it I'll never get enough again.'

'One minute you're prepared to leave him to fend for himself, the next you're rushing to pay his debts.'

'I married him. I can't just conveniently forget it.'

'How you stick by the conventions,' he said quietly, 'the absolute letter of duty.'

I walked on, down the sloping street. Beyond the landing stage and the wharves was blankness; no river, no sky, no distant shore; only a space of what looked like dirty steam.

'There's Ian,' he said suddenly, 'coming out of Skinner's.'

He hadn't seen us. He was hurrying, back to the office I

supposed, since he was wearing his glasses. I almost started after him; but what had I to say?

'Aren't you going to ask his brotherly sympathy?' said Hedley. 'I thought that must have been why you came down here.'

'Leave me alone. You with your sarcasms, you think you know everything, you don't understand.'

We reached the open space at the end of the road. Slanting rain lashed our faces. I ran towards the pier entrance. The clock on the streaming buff boards above the booking office said two minutes to ten. The ferry was due to leave, they would be pulling up the gangways. There wouldn't be another for fifteen minutes.

'Where are you going?' he said.

'Nowhere. I don't know. Sometimes I just go on the ferry to the other side, then come back. It makes a change.'

I took off my rain-blurred glasses and wiped them.

'Agnes.' He put his hand on my elbow and held it. 'Shall we go up to London?'

'Now?' Astonishment made me sound dismayed.

'Well no, Monday's not a very bright day. Perhaps Wednesday. We'll ask Tom. Unless you can't forgive me anyway.'

'Forgive what?'

'The test.'

He wasn't teasing, wasn't even smiling.

'It isn't your fault,' I said. 'You told me dozens of times to look in the mirror.'

He moved his hand on my arm. 'We shouldn't have stopped so often to talk. Will you come, then?'

Would I come! All I had to think about was restraining myself from an unseemly snatch. 'Yes,' I said, 'I'll come. Thank you.'

He smiled. 'You've swallowed your medicine, now you can have a sweet.'

It was hard to be reminded of my schoolgirl status; but I was willing to accept any terms. 'I thought you'd have made such a tough parent,' I said, 'not the kind that rushes to placate a child with lollies.'

'I should be like most parents, fond, human, and fallible.' He dropped his hand from my arm, and for a moment I saw no masculine carapace, only a person who happened to be a man, capable of being hurt, who looked as if some thought or circumstance had temporarily defeated him. I wanted to lean my head on his shoulder, hold his hand, touch his furrowed cheek: clumsy inadequate offerings of sympathy that were all I knew. But I couldn't touch him, any more than I could stroke Ian's forehead when he had a headache. There was nothing I could do for either of them, except leave them alone.

'Are you tired?' he said.

'You're not used to seeing me without these.' I put on my glasses.

'That's better. Do you want to cross on the next ferry? Or shall we go home?'

I thought for a moment. 'You take the car. I'll come back by bus. I'd better have my hair done unless you want to take a drowned rat to London.'

'I did say mouse,' he murmured, holding out his hand to test the rainfall, which had almost stopped. 'I'll wait for you. I have to see about getting some gas delivered. Where is your hairdresser's?'

'Keppel Street, the next one up from here.'

'I'll come with you, see where to bring the car. It may be raining again when you come out. You won't want to ruin the morning's work walking up to Lansdowne Road.'

'How good you are to me. Better than I ever deserve.'

'You're easily pleased. Besides, I make allowances. That's something you don't know how to do.'

We walked by the river to the foot of Keppel Street. It was the part of Shayle I liked best, where in the late eighteenth century someone in abortive ambition had laid out a few streets and squares, of which this was the best, built to take advantage of the sloping shore and the prospect of the river. From the foot of the hill the eye came to rest on a statue of Butcher Cumberland, the reason for which strange choice Tom had once told me, and I repeated to Hedley. Thus in calm discussion of Shayle and architecture the moment of weakness and tenderness passed, as moments invariably do: but they leave their scars, their subtle changes, and imperceptibly they mount up.

There was a sunburst window over the hairdresser's door. The area rails were painted pale blue, to match the elegant iron balcony that curved out from the first floor windows.

'No wonder you like coming here,' he said. 'How long will it take to transform you?'

Mouse. It was the nearest thing to a term of endearment I had to treasure. I hardened my heart. 'I'll tell her to make me extra sophisticated.'

'Go on then,' he said with a smile, '*étonne-moi*.'

'All right, I will. Give me till one o'clock.'

I had no appointment, but it was Monday, the easiest time of all, and I'd been one of her best customers for nearly six years. She said if I could give her fifteen minutes she could give me the rest of the morning, and offered me a sheaf of magazines. But in that fifteen minutes I went out and bought a bottle of Amour Amour.

It began to rain again as I came back. I was already wet, but it pelted hard. I ran for shelter into the narrow covered passage that leads between the first two houses of Keppel Street to an alley at the back; a dark entrance, down three steps, smelling musty and faintly lavatorial. I stood on the bottom step, wiped my glasses, and watched the rain, occasionally sniffing at my wrist where as a formality I'd dabbed perfume.

Someone came up the passage behind me, running. I stood to one side. The footsteps stopped. I supposed whoever it was had seen the rain. Then I remembered that there was no other entrance to the passage except from the open alley, where presumably it rained as hard as in the street. I turned round. Sankton was standing behind me.

'Hullo,' I said, too surprised to stop. His coffee-cream skin was wet, he was breathing rather fast. He must have run some way.

'You,' he said. 'I didn't know you.' He grinned at my hair. 'Been for a dip in the river, duck?'

'What are *you* doing?' I said coldly.

'My flat's along the road.' He looked quickly up and down the street. 'You on your own?'

I treated him to a frigid stare. His shallow grey eyes returned one just as hard; but in the end he softened first.

'You don't know a thing, do you?' he said, shaking his head with incomprehensible pity. He came close. His head was level with my shoulder; he was about an inch shorter than me and I was standing on the step. 'I like you, plain Jane,' he said. 'You never let me down that time. Lots of women would have talked, even whined at their husbands to come up and make a stink over nothing.'

He stared without shame into my eyes. There were raindrops on his thick lashes. 'Got anything on your conscience?' he said softly.

I turned away, because I was both bewildered and conscious of guilt.

'Well watch it,' he went on. 'Someone's had their eye on you a long time. I tried to do you a good turn once before, but I don't think you'd see what was under your nose.'

'I don't know what you're talking about.'

'I know you don't, that's why I'm telling you,' he said impatiently. 'Mind what you say in future and who you say it to. You don't know what they've done to me, your blue-eyed boy and your prim little husband. One goes creep and the other goes telltale tit to the part-time boss. And I suppose your pious brother-in-law gives spiritual guidance.'

I turned round, furious. He was staring past me, down the street. 'Keep your lid on,' he said quickly, 'I'm going.' He moved up two steps and stood above me. 'Good luck, kid. Don't play safe on his grey hair. He'd have had young Livia flat if she hadn't warned him off.'

He leaned across and kissed me, pinning my arms against the wall with his hands. It was so quick I hardly had time to react. He moved back, and with gentle unerring delicacy drew his hands over my breasts.

'You're lovely,' he said. 'Make the most of it.'

He ran across the pavement into the road. On the far side a car was slowing down, and although it didn't stop as he reached it he slipped in the back and slammed the door, and the car accelerated to turn left at the lights, which were green, into the London road. All that, I saw, before I turned round, leaning on the wall, facing the dark passage to calm down and get back my breath.

I didn't understand his mysteries, his oblique hints. What had they done to him, Tom and Hedley? What good turn had he tried to do me? I didn't know; but I sensed tension, resentment, things that had happened over my head. Only his insults were clear to me, and his boundless opportunist audacity. Plain Jane. I pressed my hands against my breast, thankful that the rain had emptied the street. No one would have seen what had happened. I turned round.

Hedley was standing on the top step. The blue-eyed boy, the grey head; he who would have had young Livia flat. He'd seen us. He'd seen everything. Those pain-blue eyes, I thought they must see through my pocket and the wrappings right to the bottle of Amour Amour.

'I was making a phone call,' he said.

There were two telephone kiosks not a dozen yards away at the corner of the road. He would have looked straight through the side.

He came down the steps. 'You might have given your rendezvous in a prettier place.' He sniffed. 'The smell of the Age of Elegance.'

I was still standing with my hands pressed under my breast. He glanced down. 'What are you doing, keeping it warm for him? He'll be gone a long time.'

I lowered my hands and stared at the floor, dumb, stupid sullen; the face I'd offered to matron, who hated you to snivel.

'No wonder you hanker for Bath and Edinburgh,' he said. 'You should have lived in the eighteenth century. Noble façades, ravishing prospects, stinking tenement slums, man deified, beauty romanticized, elegance at a premium—and every so often a mutiny, a rebellion, an upsurge of the rabble. Yes, down at the bottom there's all the low life you'd like to deny but can't, the moulds, the bacteria, the fungi, the muddy teeming marsh that will outlive you, the life that will go on, neither reason nor romance. You despise it but you can't escape, you have to succumb, time and again. The electrician's mate, the married man, Sankton—'

'I didn't. Not Sankton. You must have seen I didn't ask for it. Why didn't you come and stop him if you disapproved?'

'He didn't give me much time.'

He lit a cigarette; and after a minute I looked at my watch.

'Twenty past. I'm due at the hairdresser's.'

'I thought you hadn't been able to get in.'

With these commonplaces we announced a truce. For a time we would pretend that nothing had happened. The rain had slightly eased, and from sheer habit we walked out together.

There was a blue car along the road, a Jag, like Tubby's. I looked at the number. It *was* Tubby's. Hedley was looking at it, naturally.

'Everyone's come to Shayle this morning,' I said. 'Whatever can Tubby be doing?'

'Look where it's parked.'

There were geraniums in the window boxes; inside, pastel Venetian blinds, full drawn, so that the black lettering on the glass stood out clearly. TURF ACCOUNTANTS.

'You don't miss much,' I said, 'I suppose you're keeping in practice.'

We stopped outside the hairdresser's.

'What do you mean?'

'Tubby thought you must be a spy. You'd certainly make a good one.'

He looked down the wide street to the river, where tugs floated like shadows in the rain. 'One o'clock,' he said. 'I'll be here.'

I went upstairs. A new girl took my coat. I sat down and stared at myself in the mirror: freckles on pallor, glasses, a lank baby octopus dropped on my skull. The schoolgirl. The mouse.

My hairdresser came and stood behind the chair. 'What do you want done?' she asked, putting her head on one side.

Caution, risks, rebukes: to hell with the lot. You're lovely, make the most of it. I closed my eyes.

'Bleach it,' I said. 'Make me blonde.'

I came out early. The street sparkled in sunshine, a perspective of flat houses, a greyer maritime Bloomsbury framing a glittering river that was almost blue. I stood in the sun and watched a liner pass. The marsh on the far shore was flattered by distance, emerald at the water's edge, tawny above.

Hedley came at five to. He hadn't put down the hood of the car, thinking perhaps that the wind would play havoc with my hair. He came round to stand on the pavement, looking at his watch. I didn't move for a moment. It was weeks since I'd seen him in all the formality of a jacket, a tie, and a white shirt; when he'd driven me to the test he'd kept on the shining black mac. He was looking towards Cumberland Place. I walked up to him, and touched his arm.

It was slow, so painfully slow, the change from blankness to reaction; slow, and barely change. He didn't smile, didn't speak, didn't even move his eyes; and in so far as there was an expression in them it was recognition, but not of me. Then came the frown, the doubt, the wariness. This was what I'd risked. I'd staked and lost.

Someone had to speak first. 'Don't you like it?' I said.

'It's all one to me, lass.'

Hedley, Hedley, I did it for you, to dazzle you; and that was all you could say.

I turned to the car.

'Wait,' he said, 'here comes your husband. Aren't you going to let him see you?'

It was no great miracle of observation to have picked out Tom's slight figure, with its odd gait, bent forward rather stiffly from the hips. He seemed to be in a hurry, though he was glancing at an evening paper. The breeze ruffled his black hair, brushed sideways in an ungainly bush. He was bound to see us, he would pass within a yard.

It wasn't so bad, at first, as I'd expected. He looked annoyed, but in an abstracted way, as if at some minor irritation, the last straw of a morning that had gone badly at work.

'Hullo,' I said, 'I've failed.'

'Bad luck,' he said mechanically. 'You'll have to try again.'

'I didn't look enough in the mirror.'

'I called to see you at the museum,' Hedley said quickly, 'but you were out.'

'I had to go down to the University library.'

I couldn't help smiling. 'You always find an indispensable bit of restful research to do when you've been bird watching.'

Hedley's mouth turned down at the corners, the castor oil smile that I could never understand. 'How did Ian survive the night?' he said.

'He's got a bad headache, he didn't come in.'

'But we *saw* him,' I said, 'coming out of Skinner's.'

Tom was silent.

'We also saw Tubby.' Hedley looked at the betting shop. 'He had to put something on Kiltartan, no doubt.'

'I believe he said Kiltartan wouldn't stay,' Tom said absently. I thought he'd turned rather pale.

'May I take your wife to London on Wednesday?'

'Certainly, she'll be very pleased.' Tom glanced at his watch.

'She'll be quite safe with me,' Hedley went on with no trace of smile. 'Safe as with her brother.' He paused. '*Would* you let her go with Ian?'

So he was capable of cruelty, the dirty kick. It didn't surprise me. I'd never imagined that he'd gone through life like an angel.

'What do you mean?' said Tom.

His indignation was too comprehending, he should have aimed at bewilderment. But if he'd known Hedley as I did he'd never had tried to bluff, to hope for escape.

'He knows,' I said wearily.

'Do you mean to say you've told him?'

'Of course she hasn't.' Hedley sounded quite angry, frightening me. 'I've got eyes, I can see for myself.'

Tom stared down the river, defeated. He tried so hard to shut it out of his life. 'How long?' he said. 'When did you see it?'

'Depends what you mean by it. I saw the likeness the first time they were together. When Fellowes explained who was who, I concluded it was coincidence, an extreme case of type resemblance, though that took some swallowing. Also at first I thought you and Ian were full brothers. Then I learnt about the orphanage. More doubts. But of course with no one acknowledging anything, I just had to puzzle on. Only this morning I saw what I'd never seen before. Ian in glasses and Agnes with fair hair. Not together, but close enough.'

Tom turned to me. 'You ask for trouble, Agnes, absolutely court it, I simply can't understand. Why did you do it? You might have thought of Ian. He's got enough worries, God knows, without adding you.'

'You mean Ian doesn't know?' Hedley said.

'No. And don't tell him.' Tom looked along the street. 'Damnation, there's Osborne. Get in the car, Agnes, I don't want him to see us.'

Mutiny rose in me. 'What does it matter? Am I going to spend my time dodging your colleagues and the neighbours, or are you going to shut me up till the bleach has grown out?'

Hedley opened the door and tipped back the seat. I don't know how they moved, but between them they hustled me into a position where without making a fuss I could do nothing but get in the back of the car. Tom sat quickly in the passenger seat and slammed the door, Hedley went round to the other side, trapping me.

'Men!' I said, trembling with rage and misery. 'How brave you are. How you stick together.'

'Agnes, if you can't be reasonable at least be quiet,' said Tom. 'You don't know what you're doing. Now shut up.'

It wasn't quite anger in his voice: vexation. Even so I'd never provoked it before. We lived together without quarrels, even if only in the cottage, he provided for me, for whatever obscure promptings still he'd married a nameless bastard which few men I suppose would care to do, he was a schoolboy but he was gentle, he'd looked after me when I had 'flu, he let me keep the kitten, he suffered me, I didn't love him, but he was my husband.

'I'm sorry,' I muttered.

Hedley offered Tom a cigarette, forgetting that neither

of us smoked. He lit one for himself. 'When did *you* see this, before or after you married her?'

'Don't be ridiculous,' said Tom.

'But it would have been no barrier, none at all. There's no blood between you. Then you saw it from the same cause as I did—bleached hair, a couple of years ago?'

He remembered everything, everything.

Tom looked startled. 'Who told you?'

'Agnes. But other people will have noticed unaided what's so plain. Tubby I'm sure, perhaps Helen. Fellowes once said to me *you might take them for brother and sister.* People don't throw out remarks like that simply to pass the time of day, they're casting to see if you'll rise to the bait.' He paused. 'Have you proved anything? Can you?'

Tom shook his head. 'I've tried. I don't know if you've any idea of the difficulties. To start, you can't force parents to put their true names to the birth register, even any name. Her mother used the name of a Yorkshire town, perhaps her own, perhaps no more than the first place to come to her head. If only it had all happened a few years later, when there was the business of identity cards and ration books to get round. Still, the hospital records gave me the mother's address in Shayle at the time of birth. She'd been living about five months in a hostel in Sion Place. I went to the social service people, the moral welfare. They had records, right back, even some people who'd worked for them twenty-five years, but of course they couldn't remember one among so many. All their information was in the file—name, age, no place of origin but Yorkshire accent, well-informed girl, capable, determined to keep child, family just a query of course, estimated skilled artisan class, small private means of undisclosed source.'

'Perhaps from the father,' said Hedley. 'I mean Agnes's father.'

'Possibility. Probably. Otherwise why come to Shayle—oh God knows. Anyway she moved to an address in Cambridge Road. I went there, but the people had only taken the house a couple of years before and didn't know the previous owners. I traced them—God, the trouble! neighbours, electoral rolls, hours of it—found the father of this family living in Paignton with a married son. Agnes's mother had taken a room with them in Shayle, went out to work at a bookshop in the High Street, and his wife looked after the baby with her own children. The wife's sister was one of the helpers at the hostel, that's how it had come about. He said she was a nice girl, very independent, very quiet. That was all. Except of course what we knew already, that she caught influenza and pneumonia when Agnes was two and died in Shayle hospital.'

'What about the bookshop?' said Hedley.

'Gone. There's a radio and television shop in its place. The manager told me where the old owner used to bank. I wrote through them. He remembered her, knew her circumstances but nothing of her background, he'd never known her by any other name. In those days you could get insurance cards over the post office counter and start from scratch, no need to produce a previous card or number or birth certificate, just fill in from the present moment. Even if she'd been in insured employment before there'd have been no way of checking. It was done through approved societies, and if your insurance lapsed no one bothered, chased you, queried it. Incredible. And that was all. She died. The hospital just had the facts as before, admission, death, and cause. If she asked for anyone it didn't find its way to the records. The orphanage only knew as much as I've told you.'

'And how she came to them,' said Hedley. 'Surely the Paignton man knew that too? Who arranged it?'

'Stenlock's, solicitors in Culham.'

'The ones who dealt with the money. That was your most promising line to the father. And Stenlock's are Ian's solicitors, he mentioned it one evening in The Ship.'

'Ian consults them from time to time, he doesn't retain them. His father did. It's no proof, they have hundreds of clients.'

Hedley pulled a face. 'And all you'd meet with solicitors would be the blank wall of professional confidence.'

'Exactly. It hardly seems reasonable. Ian's father's dead, old Stenlock who would have promised secrecy, he's dead too. But no. Anything undertaken in confidence must stay wrapped up for all time.'

'When did Ian's father die?'

'Eight years ago, before I met her.'

'So he was still alive when Agnes had the money. It was a gift. If it had been in his will of course you'd have seen it, sorry.' He paused. '*Your* mother, is she still alive?'

'She lives with my aunt in Scarborough.'

'You come from Yorkshire, I keep forgetting. So did Agnes's mother.'

'I know. It was—a bond between us, when we first knew each other.' He gave me a rather woebegone smile. 'He might have met them both about the same time. His work took him a lot about the country.'

'When you finally suspected, you set to work on your own, didn't tell her what you were looking for?'

'I hoped it might come to nothing.'

'Why tell her in the end?'

'I thought she should know.'

'Why not Ian?'

'For God's sake, how would you like someone to come up and say *here's a bastard of your honoured father's, born eight months after he married his second wife?* Do you think Ian's father comes out of it very well?'

'You might excuse eight more than ten. What was he like, Ian's father?'

'How can I say, looking back now? I suppose—he was like Ian.' Tom brushed his hand across his hair, as if he were trying to flatten it; a sign of worry, agitation. 'God Almighty, who do people ever—'

He broke off pressing his lips together, and glanced at his watch. 'I must go,' he said shortly. 'This is my lunch hour.'

He didn't have to rush about to the pressure of a clock, he could come and go more or less as he pleased, though he rarely did. His haste was an excuse to avoid talking or if possible thinking of what gave him so much uneasiness.

'Will it save time if we take you?' Hedley asked.

'No, thanks. I want to see Skinner about some books first.' He looked confused, as if realizing too late the discrepancy between his last two sentences. 'Agnes, just do one thing for me. Stay in for a bit. I don't know what to do, I'll have to think. Give me time.'

'All right,' I said.

He turned to Hedley. 'Perhaps you'd come down this evening.'

'I will if you like, but it's nothing to do with me. I shan't say anything.'

'Then why did you?' I asked.

Tom opened the door. 'My dear, you'd better get used to people being unable to contain their curiosity. You were lucky to escape before, I don't know how you did.'

'It was short and curly before,' I said miserably. 'Perhaps it's the smoothness–'

But Tom had got out and shut the door.

Hedley lit another cigarette. 'Well, well,' he said, 'this is a pretty caper.' He opened the door and tipped forward the seat. 'Come and sit beside me, I can't talk to you back there. You don't want to drive, do you?'

I shook my head and moved to the front. He didn't start the car, simply sat there smoking.

'What have you been up to, Agnes?' he said after a while.

'Sankton asked me that, or something like it. Why?'

'Someone's watching you.'

'What do you mean?' I was puzzled and slightly alarmed. 'You and Sankton—who's watching me? Where?'

'Don't stare. He's in the porch of the tailor's farther up the street. There are mirror panels with gold lettering set at an angle down the sides of the entrance. He can see us in the glass. I've been watching him some time.'

'In that case perhaps he's watching *you* with suspicion, waiting to see if he need phone the police.'

'He is police, plain clothes. C.I.D.'

'How do you know?' I said, frightened by his quiet certainty. 'Are you one. *Were* you?'

'No,' he said. He frowned, as if reproving his own vehemence. 'Whatever you've done, his suspicion will be doubled now that you've coloured your hair.'

'But I've done nothing.' I hesitated. 'Sankton said *someone's had their eye on you a long time.*'

He smiled. 'He didn't mean the C.I.D. Anyway let's give him a run for his money.'

He started the car and pulled out quickly from the van that was parked in front of us. The man in the tailor's porch didn't look up as we passed. The lights were green, we turned into Cumberland Place, the London road.

'*If* they want to follow you, they will,' he said. 'You know that, of course. You won't shake them off.'

'If they do it's a mistake. I've nothing on my conscience.'

He glanced at me. 'Not even Ian? Don't look so appalled. It wouldn't have been your fault when you didn't know. I thought perhaps that was why Tom had so unnecessarily told you, to put the brakes on.'

'I think he had to talk to someone. As for Ian, I told you, I don't steal. I don't deny I always liked him. How could I help it? He's so nice.'

'Nice! Certainly he's nice. He's inherited great charm, especially for women, no doubt.'

'Can't you understand? I know we can't be sure, nothing can ever be proved. But it meant so much to me, just the possibility. A brother, even a half brother, something I'd never thought I'd have, a relation. I wanted to tell everyone, especially Ian, you don't know how I wanted.'

'Yes, he's handsome and intelligent enough to meet with your approval. If he were one of the absolute nits you wouldn't be so ready to own him.' He pulled up at Trinity crossroads. 'I'm going round the back ways. If there is anything behind us we'll shake it off.'

The red light blurred, diluted with amber, a pendant drop of juice squeezed from a fruit. He turned left.

'I think it probably *is* true,' he said. 'There are the circumstances of Yorkshire, and Shayle, and the solicitor. But most of all I'd rely on the likeness between you. Even your characters are similar.'

'I thought environment determined character more than heredity.'

'Your environments weren't so different. He lost his mother, his father was often away and then remarried. You were in the *good* home, with the *nice* orphans. Quite a fair balance, I think. Whatever the cause, background or heredity, you're both what Tubby calls suckers for looks. You know your own side of it. Think of Ian. The photographs, the colour slides, the flowers, walking half a mile up Culham High Street rather than sit facing a teashop's hideous murals, the Gauguin girl on the office wall. Yes, and you both tried to ignore it in favour of some forced notion of duty when you married. At least I can't conceive that Helen ever possessed the slightest physical attraction, sexual, aesthetic or anything else, which is one reason I'm sorry for her. As for you—you've told me yourself how you married.'

He was gentle, in spasms, it was part of what I feared in him. He smoothed over what Sankton had ripped apart: *your prim little husband.* Tom wasn't ugly, wasn't even plain, he wasn't, for all Sankton's sneer, so very little; but he was slight, and awkward, and undeniably odd-looking with his bushy black hair and his stiff walk; and although I was ashamed that these things should matter to me, though I repeated like a litany his qualities, his attributes, his quiet worth, yet I often longed in despair to do what I had done years ago, lean on someone tall and bend back to be kissed, not down.

'What is Tom's mother like?' he asked.

I started. 'Oh—homely, ordinary.'

He nodded. 'Perhaps Ian's father remarried sensibly, to get someone to look after the home, the cooking, Ian.'

'More likely a measure to keep himself out of trouble. Only my mother was the last to succumb. He might have married *her* if he'd known in time.'

'He'd have done just as well. The nice quiet independent girl, determined to keep the child. Living testimony. Didn't it console you?'

He pulled the car into the side of the road and switched off the engine. We were in a quiet street in the outskirts of Shayle.

'Do you really believe you know nothing of your parents? At least they recognized responsibility, did what they could to repair the damage. At least there was respect between them. Otherwise she'd never have kept that silence right to the end.'

I was grateful to him. He tried to put it all in the best possible light, the way I should have liked to believe it had happened. And after all, it was not impossible. There was no need to rake over the muddy chances of rape, blackmail, recrimination, those morbid nightmares of my late teens, they hardly fitted the facts: the charm that Ian had inherited, the character of my mother, her willingness to keep me. At worst I was conceived in casualness; one of millions, in or out of wedlock.

'He was in Wales when she died,' I said. 'We checked it with Tom's mother, working round with questions about how much he'd been away. He wouldn't have known unless she wrote, and I don't suppose she was able.'

'He might have taken you himself.'

'I suppose it would have been worse for him to admit paternity after so long. If he suggested adoption it would look too suspicious to insist on a child with a squint. And if he was the source of this vast visual-aesthetic weakness you see in me and Ian he wouldn't want to. My mother must have been quite good looking. Just my luck to take after him.'

'Ian's very handsome.'

'He's a man. Besides, I'm not his living image.'

'You're not far off it now.'

'Of course the money might have come from her relations,' I said quickly, because he was looking at me so hard. 'They didn't want embarrassment, the scandal at home.'

'Not so likely as the other. She didn't mention relations. Perhaps they'd quarrelled. Perhaps she was an orphan herself.'

'You mean, like me? The endless chain of heredity, blood will out. You're as bad as Helen with her broken homes. Oh, what does it matter now? We'll never know.'

'Do you remember what you said about the men? People *manage to do the things they really want.* I think it might be possible to prove more. Tom did well single-handed, but if you were to engage—'

'What? Genealogists?'

'Private detectives. A large firm would do it, I think.'

'My God! All the scum that drifts round the divorce courts, picking scabs off people's lives. Tom would never consider it. Anyway it would be too expensive and you know he's short of money.'

'I suppose so,' he said quietly. He started the car.

'Besides, he'd have to face it all over again,' I said. 'Ian's father might have warned him that I existed.'

'You've no common blood. As long as Ian was safely married there was nothing to guard against.'

'No, technically. But it's a shock when you discover that the man whom from the age of five you've called father may have fathered your wife. You know it's all right but it takes some getting used to.' I paused. 'Even that's not so hard as the next step—the million to one chance of his picking on me.'

'Once your mother came to Shayle the rest isn't so

amazing. Deal out heredity and environment as we did and universal education will do the rest. You can say *if only I hadn't gone to the historical society, if only Tom weren't interested in the archaeology of the estuary, if only he hadn't come back to do a thesis*—but there's no end to that. If only your mother hadn't lived in Yorkshire, if only Ian's father hadn't been a civil engineer. You can peel back time to the Garden of Eden just to settle your personal account. But once Tom did meet you—'

'What was the attraction of the lanky freckled bespectacled mouse-haired bastard all wrapped up in another man? Oh, he could answer as well as you can. The living image of the hero-brother, conveniently feminine. It was quite natural that he should be attracted, consciously or not. He says not. Tom's very patient, very stolid. He dealt with it as he would some ecological experiment, or a problem at work, the way he went about his inquiries, methodically, rationally. It was simply a question of adjusting his mind. He had no religion to complicate matters for him. All the same—' I hesitated. 'It made a difference to us. Don't imagine anything too drastic. Just a general inhibition.'

'You didn't get quite the steady emotionless refuge you married for.'

'Go on,' I said. 'Say it serves me right. I shan't dispute.'

He was silent. We drove along the Roman road, fairly quiet in the lunch hour. Steam was curling off the glittering tarmac.

'I don't look enough in the mirror,' I repeated. 'If that examiner knew just how I've scrutinized myself, trying to see this likeness that's supposed to be so strong.'

'What you see staring back from a mirror isn't what everyone else sees. No one can ever see himself.'

'You said so many pointed things to me about Ian, even heredity. Sometimes I thought you must have guessed. I suppose they were just casual remarks, the point was in my knowledge.'

'I don't make many casual remarks,' he said with inexplicable bitterness. 'They're just not all framed as questions. I suffer from curiosity the way some people suffer from migraine. How you've tormented it, with Ian, the way you look at him, speak to him. No one else brings that light in your eyes, you give yourself away. Only I couldn't make out what you gave away. I thought it was your mother's warm heart coming out in you, that you'd like to add him to the score.'

I sighed. 'I've told you, I'm very fond of Ian—'

'Don't do such violence to my intelligence and Ian's charm and your own honesty. You love him, you idolize him, you absolutely adore him. Oh, I know, love, say that and you lift the lid off a dustbin. Parent and child, brother and sister, man and woman, childhood friends, none of them can bear scrutiny below the top level, one vast incestuous blood-sucking knot of vipers. The only thing to do is lift up the lid, take a look, say *bless my soul, the whole thing's a nest of vipers*, and carry on, which is what Tom tries to do, I suppose. I'm not accusing, judging, condemning, I'm just stating what I can see, making allowance for the tainted source of every single tender feeling, the vipers that are not our responsibility, taking a discarded discredited natural standard. You love him. Don't you? More than anyone else in the world.'

'Yes,' I said. 'Yes, I do.'

'Good girl,' he said quietly. 'You join me. I had brothers.'

We turned into the drive. Sankton's garage seemed to be closed. There were no cars at the pumps, but a woman was standing in the forecourt, staring about her. She had frizzy bleached hair and a vulpine face tanned dry by the sun. That unfamiliar brownness delayed my recognition until Hedley had turned into the chalk-pit path.

'Would you stop?' I said. 'I want to go back to the garage.'

He gave me an odd look as he pulled up. 'Why?'

'Didn't you see that woman from the stocking counter, Livia's ex-landlady? She might have some message, or letter to send on—I don't know, I couldn't help, but I think I'll go and see. No one seems to be about up there. If you want to go on, do. I'll walk down.'

He got out of the car and came with me, however, through the gap between the sheds to the cinder patch, where I'd seen him so long before, sweating over his car in the heat of a Sunday afternoon. The doors of the sheds were all open.

'Someone must be here,' I said. 'Where's your car?'

'I left it down by The Ship last night.'

'But I saw you take it away after the picnic.'

'I brought it back.'

'Why?'

We had come round to the front, and the woman was walking away. I ran after her.

'Did you come about Livia?' I said.

She turned on me. 'So she *has* shown up here?'

'She's left, you know that,' I said, reacting sharply. 'She's changed her job.'

Her eyes registered half recognition of my face. I suppose to her I was fifteen denier stretch seamless size C long.

'I don't know about that,' she said aggressively. 'All I know—'

'Just a minute,' I cut in. 'My sister-in-law called at your house weeks ago to ask about Livia. I took her in my car. I think you'll remember that.' It cost me an effort to acknowledge Helen, but I disliked this woman.

'Well I knew she'd gone,' she said defensively. 'I just wondered if she'd been round here, or if anyone knew where I could find her. Only I get back from my holiday this morning and what do I find? Someone's been and taken a pile of linen out of my drawers.'

'Are you accusing Livia?'

'She knew where to find it.'

'Any fool of a burglar might know what to find in a chest of drawers.'

'What else is missing?' Hedley said quietly.

Her eyes darted at him and flickered away again, quick as a snake's tongue. 'Nothing,' she said. 'If there was burglars they'd have taken more. No, she found herself a bit short at her new place and come and helped herself, that's what.'

'Went to the trouble and danger of breaking in to steal a few towels and sheets,' he observed.

'No, well,' she said evasively, 'she could have got in. She never gave back the key, went off with it.'

She couldn't meet the look Hedley levelled at her, not that I was surprised. Helen had been quick to distrust her honesty, and for once she seemed justified.

'Why don't you go to the police?' Hedley asked.

'Well, I don't want to be hard on the girl,' she said, shifting to hypocrisy. 'I thought I'd find her, give her a good talking to.'

'You won't find her here,' he said. 'She's been left weeks, no one knows where she's gone. And if you go round making unsubstantiated allegations you'll get no one into trouble but yourself. Either go to the police or shut up, clear out and forget it.'

This mild reproof was delivered in an accent rougher and more clipped than he'd ever used to me. The woman went without a word, shooting me a vindictive look.

'I'll never buy stockings in Denning's again,' I said. 'Something odd there. What do you think?'

'I can't think for hunger,' he said shortly. 'Come on.'

We went back to the cinders. By the door of one of the sheds a man was standing, not one of Sankton's men so far as I knew; he didn't look at all like a garage worker, with his quiet blue suit. He glanced at Hedley; just once, but I saw that he knew him.

'Who was that? One of your C.I.D. friends?'

'Avon security.'

'But Sankton isn't an Avon agent.' I stopped short at the sight of the car. 'Did *you* do that?'

The white paint was marked on the off-side by a long straight scratch and a series of parallel lighter lines like combing, as if the car had been scraped along a projecting brick.

'You failed the test, not me.'

'I didn't touch a thing,' I said. 'How could I miss the kind of bump that did that? You know my steering was good.'

'Yes, hairbreadth,' he said coldly. 'Brinkmanship, the razor's edge, the narrow squeak, you're a great expert in that line. Anyway that was already there this morning. You must have been too worked up to notice it. I concluded you'd taken it out last night for a trial run.'

'Alone, in the dark? Are you mad? Or do you think I am?'

'I heard it come past the caravan. I didn't sleep well, I'd gone to bed too early, having no light.'

'That must have been Tom coming back from Lindhurst.'

'No. I heard him later, about half-past two.'

'He must have come in and gone out again. I didn't wake, I'd taken aspirins to make sure I slept. He probably couldn't resist going to see what those ornithologists were up to. Don't you know that nothing's beyond him where the marsh is concerned?'

'I suppose so,' he said. 'You always make sure the hand-brake's on when you leave it in the garage, and block the wheels? There's a slope all the way to the street.'

'My life's not going to be worth living from now on. You'd never have dared ask me that before I failed.'

He dragged the toe of his shoe across the tyres; chalk lay in the treads, like white marbling. 'Sorry,' he said.

We got in the car. He took off the brake and let the car coast down the path, a thing he'd never allowed me to do.

'You've still no gas,' I said as we passed the caravan. 'Do you want to come down to the kitchen to cook?'

'Too much trouble, thanks. I'll have bread and cheese at The Ship.'

He turned the wheel suddenly and very quickly, swinging the car in front of the garage shed. He got it half in, at a slant, before the slope of the ground stopped it. He pulled up the brake.

'I thought not,' he said. 'You have to be quite a skilled driver even to get it this far without the engine.'

'How vain you are.'

'Preach vanity to me when I've had *my* hair dyed.'

'You wouldn't,' I said, 'You know damn well—'

'Go on. What do I know damn well?'

Why had they spoilt me, the electrician's mate, the married man, Tom? sought me out, leaving me inexperienced of the hunt, unable to turn a moment to advantage.

'It suits you,' I said lamely.

He raised his eyebrows. 'The vipers are wriggling furiously this morning. First the brother, now the parent substitute.'

'Can't you take anything at face value?'

He looked in the driving mirror. 'That *is* face value. Shall I start the engine? Or shall we get out and push?'

'Is verbal communication possible with you? That unfortunate woman, she probably never meant to say no. Why don't you ask her again?'

'You're very generous with what you've no use for.'

'I don't like you—not to have what you want,' I said.

'Don't sound so serious, it doesn't suit you.'

He'd had twenty years longer than me to learn, he was weathered and battered by heartbreaking, active and passive, he was a rock. I'd glimpsed faults, weaknesses, cracks of gentleness; but not on the bleak north face that I was trying hopelessly to scale barehanded, lacking the irons of sophistication.

He moved the car to its proper position. I picked up Tom's discarded newspaper, got out and put the bricks under the wheels. Then we walked down the path together, I to the cottage, he making for the street and The Ship.

'What would you do if I *were* serious?' I said.

'Run like hell.'

'Just like a man.'

'I am a man.'

Ah, Hedley, get away! My whole infatuation was with his unasserted taken-for-granted masculinity. I had to accept it whole, not selectively, the callousness with the strength; and in spite of the raised eyebrow and dry smile what I saw in his blue eyes was alarm, anxiety, dread of entanglement. I thought of the losses that had gouged those lines in his face;

parents, brothers, heartbreaks, the one who'd said no. He'd suffered enough.

'Don't worry,' I said. 'I'm not serious.'

'Just feminine.'

We had reached the cottage. He walked on. I opened the kitchen door. Mittens stood up, stretched, and ran forward to meet me.

I changed my driving test suit for the first old cotton dress that came to hand, which happened to be the one I had been wearing when Sankton made the pass, short, straight, sleeveless. Then I went down to get Mittens his much delayed lunch. He rubbed into my legs as I cut it up, uttering the rasping sounds that are caused by mewing and purring together; but I hadn't the heart to talk to him.

I put down the plate and turned to wash my hands. Hedley was leaning against the door.

'I've never known anyone slink about like you,' I said. 'Has Fellowes run out of cheese?'

'I came back to make a verbal communication. There's a van parked by the church, and the driver's asleep at the wheel.'

'Well?'

'What kind of driver do you usually see sleeping in the cabin?'

'Lorry drivers, I suppose.'

'Yes, in heavy wagons on long-distance runs.'

'Can't the poor fellow have a nap after lunch without your suspecting he's some minion of the C.I.D.?'

'He's parked where he can watch the entrance to the chalk-pit. And he's leaning back in the corner so that he can see without appearing to open his eyes.'

'Even odder that the C.I.D. should watch just one end of the path.'

'There may be someone in the trees by Sankton's.'

'You must have a persecution complex.' I checked myself, too late of course. What did we know of him? Was this a relapse from mental convalescence?

'Don't alarm yourself,' he said. 'I haven't. It would have been just too bad if I had.'

'I'm sorry. I didn't mean it.'

'Egoists never do. At least malice recognizes that others possess feelings, if only to be hurt.'

I tore a strip off the paper towel and dried my hands. 'Why did you say Sankton would be gone a long time?'

'There were suitcases in the back of the car, and he turned into the London road. Disappointed?'

'Someone will have to take me driving when you've gone.' Feeble bravado.

'You'd never ask Sankton. You know he'd beat you at your own game.'

'Game?' I said blankly.

He looked me up and down, a Biblical look, Authorized Version, I was wearing the Sankton dress.

'You'll get hurt one day if you go on like this,' he said.

'What have I done?'

'They didn't teach you much did they, those two little affairs you're so proud of? You don't have to do anything, just exist, just sit in the car with bare arms and short skirts slipping over the knees that Sankton couldn't bear to let pass, just turn on your melting smile and open your mouth to utter wounding stupidities. You're like the schoolgirls with their berets, only knowing half what they're asking for. Oh, you detested being treated like one. You would have taken away my line of retreat, your own defence. But it won't always be me you flirt with.'

Flirt. I picked up the dish mop and turned it over in my hands. 'You didn't have to give me lessons.'

'No, I embraced my punishment. Figuratively, of course. I didn't want to join Sankton in the deep freeze. I played by your rules. It passed a summer, didn't it? pleasantly if not very estimably for both of us. Mutual flattery, though I had the better bargain. You did more than Russian for my convalescence, Agnes. Not from illness. I just tried to recover from the snagged-up mistakes of a misspent life. The same complaint as yours. Only you were simply taking yet another aspirin.'

The kettle began to whistle; I went across the room and pulled off its cap. 'I'm sorry it's been a punishment,' I said, keeping my back to him, 'even if it was self-inflicted.'

'Too strong. Nothing worse than a trifling inconvenience.' He put a bite on trifling. 'I can pay for what I want.'

I turned round. 'As when you stayed in the night in London?'

'You have flashes of understanding.' He seemed surprised, all the same. Then his eyes changed as he looked at my hair, blonde like his heartbreak's, the one who'd said no; that wound must open every time he saw me. I hadn't meant to hurt him. Egoists never do.

'Your hair's pretty,' he said. 'It always was, you know.'

'You're so inconsistent, the way you talk to me.'

'It's the underground war. Sometimes truces, sometimes running battles.'

'What war?'

'Male and female created He them. Indispensable enemies.'

Male and female. I couldn't see that they were so different. Each callous, and apparently immature for ever, each sighting the same goal, only from different angles at different degrees; each afraid to show their hand in case the other should run.

'Why should you think I'd say no?' I turned down the gas under the kettle.

'Don't be irresponsible,' he said quietly. 'Wake up.' He pulled himself away from the door. 'I shouldn't worry about the C.I.D. Even they can't run you in for nothing at all.'

'They won't see me. Tom asked me to stay in.'

He looked at me over his shoulder as he went. 'How dutiful.'

It seemed a pity to waste the boiling water. I put some instant coffee in a cup, filled it, and sat down at the table. The sun shone through the window, making a warm patch on my shoulders. Mittens chewed raw liver with disgusting noise. Down in the street Ancrum's whistle sounded the end of the lunch hour; for a couple of minutes the street would be alive with men walking back from the Promenade and the rusty barges where they ate their sandwiches, or gliding single-pedalled on their bikes into the gate of the yard. Then the sun motes would settle round the silent Georgian houses, the decaying cottages, the blackened church. Gunfleet. Here I existed, a thoughtless egoist, an irresponsible flirt, and here I should rot, hoarding my penny treasure: your hair's pretty.

Mittens jumped on my lap, licking his chops, and made preparations for lying down. I stroked his ears as I sipped the coffee. Punishment. Wounding stupidities.

I pulled Tom's evening paper towards me; he rarely brought one back to the cottage. It was full of the usual senselessness, domestic and international, lacking even the dignity of a major disaster. But there was something for me to read, three lines squeezed in to fill the foot of a column. *Avon robbery.* Police had found the Jowett abandoned in a chalk-pit near Lawne. I turned the page. It was surprising that they'd driven so far before changing cars. Lawne was about twenty miles in, near where we'd had our picnic yesterday.

We hadn't meant to go to Lawne. The men had taken us there for a reason so flimsy it wouldn't stand up, taken us into the private field with its thistles and flies, and Tubby had said what he never would say in his senses: *ice cream:* Tubby had fobbed us off while they went in the private wood to the path with the tyre marks that led to the road. Tubby had acted patrol and whistled a warning, had kept us playing just at the edge, Tubby who followed the turf and muttered to Tom in the shade of the church, Tom who had sold his microscope and day after day drove to work with Ian, Ian who stayed at home with a splitting headache yet went into Skinner's and on Friday, wage days, played golf with Tubby, Tubby who hurried to the turf accountant, Tubby who grappled so smoothly with news of a phone call, Tubby who stopped to ring, so he said, the Lindhurst friend, arranged to listen to hypothetical nightjars with tired Ian and Tom who took his neatly manoeuvred car, Tom with unrivalled knowledge of the estuary, Tom who on Friday once a month for the past two years had wandered unquestioned over the Avon works, the patient stolid amasser of facts, the observer of patterns and change, who with Ian and Tubby had stood on a Friday in Culham beside the Avon rogue whom I'd seen at Sankton's, Sankton who hinted, suspect Sankton who'd run from the back of his flat and jumped in a moving car for the London road, this morning in Shayle where they'd all converged, where the C.I.D. had watched me, the C.I.D. who waited now at the end of the chalk-pit path—

I stood up, lifting Mittens in my arms, frightened by the surge of my thoughts. Ian, Tom, Tubby. Brother, husband, friend. The captain, the junior, the fat brainy loafer. Three able lonely disappointed men, all short of money.

It was impossible. Yet there were cases, I'd read: *I did it for the wife.* What had I done, with my Petal Dew, stockings, car? Tom hadn't mentioned the robbery, he who was so close to Avon, though he'd admitted reading of it. How abstractedly he'd walked along this morning, scanning the unaccustomed paper, how agitated he'd been. Tom. My husband. I couldn't believe it; there was too much that didn't fit. But there was too much that did.

I put Mittens on the chair. I wanted help; someone who could judge, who never flattered, the blue-eyed rock, the savage.

Hedley. Hedley who recognized Avon security, who was so quick to repudiate the police, who on Friday might have been anywhere because we had no lesson, the car was at Sankton's to be cleaned and serviced. Hedley friend of Walter, the inside link, the stranger who stayed so long, so close, in this dead end, embracing his punishment, Hedley about whom we knew nothing except that he was a man.

There had been four masked men. Three able men and a fourth.

I put Mittens on my shoulder, picked up his tray and went upstairs. I laid the tray on the floor and showed him where it was, then settled him on the bed in a patch of sunlight. He rolled over dabbing my hand with innocuous paws; it was his broken tail, his blemish, perhaps, that made him so clinging and gentle.

'Don't worry, my treasure,' I said. 'Your mistress will go out to teach, and you shall have liver and mince just the same, whatever happens, my sweet, whatever happens.'

Nothing would happen if I went to the men and said: *I've guessed.* They would stick together, hustle me into the back seat, the woman, the weakness, the time-dishonoured blabber, allow me no right to help. My only chance was to say to them: *I know.* And for that I should have to find out.

I took a clean handkerchief from the box, and my purse with the key and a couple of pound notes, kissed Mittens good-bye and shut the door. There was no one to whom I could turn, only myself to rely on. I was alone.

The palms of my hands were hot and red, covered with sticky black grit from the handlebars. I bent down and wiped them on the damp sponge of grass and moss from which raindrops hung undisturbed, in which the tyre tracks were still preserved. They would have had to open the gate to enter the ride from the road. Why should they? To transfer to their own car, already hidden there, what they had taken, and themselves, all but one who drove the Jowett to the chalk-pit? Then the tracks of the Jag or the Mini-Minor would not be found near the Jowett.

I was mad. I acknowledged it without ceasing to speculate. Why should they have waited here, why *here*? in the soft moss, the dead end, by the flint wall with its secretive little door? It was more likely that the tracks were made by a lover's car, backed into privacy and darkness.

In any case what had I hoped to achieve by coming?

What could I prove? The whole thing was so pointless I might as well go back to the cottage; so pointless I might as well go on.

There was no path along the wall, but undergrowth was sparse, chiefly low bramble. They had been gone so long yesterday afternoon on their alleged search for *Hordelymus europaea,* they must have walked further than this. Ian and Tom. Ian the soul of honour, the volunteer at Cassino, the champion of duty, the captain. And Tom, my unfortunate husband, who in spite of my faults had once so much confided in me; surely he would have come to me first if he was so short, stopped me from spending, asked me to sell the car? But three years had passed since he'd told me about Ian, three years of change, strain, and drift. He saw me more clearly, perhaps, trusted me less. The straightest people suffer aberrations, I knew that, in theory. But this was not aberration, this was planned calculated crime. Nothing spectacular; by some standards a petty snatch. Even so I couldn't believe it of Ian and Tom. But Tubby, Tubby with his debts, his gambling—

There was a broad green belt through the wood, leading from wide wooden doors in the wall beyond which a slate roof was visible. Stables, or what had once been stables, of the house on the corner, the house of big cars and big dogs which today I had not heard, the house about which Hedley had spoken so evasively. *Perhaps it's that sort of club. Gambling, licensing laws.*

Gambling. If Tubby had wanted the money, why had Ian and Tom—

All for one and one for all. The men would stick together. But was it that sort of club? Or a club at all?

The stable gates were shut tight, probably by a bar on the

inside. I turned back the way I had come. I would go in by the main gates and the lodge; and if I were stopped it would prove at least that the place had something to hide.

My bicycle rested against the fence as I'd left it, taking a chance that no one would come along the quiet lane, or that no one would be tempted by such an ancient crate, unpadlocked though it was. I closed the gate behind me and turned round. There was Hedley sitting in his car a little way up the road, looking at me without a smile.

Hedley. Hedley about whom we were to ask no questions, but who asked so many, remembered so much and so exactly, who had led me to confide our stresses and poverty, the texture of our lives, Hedley who had secretly pelted back to the tyre marks, not for the reason he'd offered: I saw that now, free from the moment's confusion: Hedley the friend of Walter, the old tried trusted army friend. Hedley the spy.

If I were to get on the bicycle and ride away he'd only come after me in the white firecracker. I leaned against the gate, resenting the unfairness of his having seen me come out, the impossibility of his having followed me along quiet lanes without my knowledge.

He let the car roll down the road, stopped it, leaned across and opened the door.

'How did you find me?' I said, without moving.

He looked at the bicycle. 'I've seen that in your garage. I just had to wait for you to come back to it.'

'How did you know where I'd gone? I didn't see you. There was no one—'

'There *is* no one, I've noticed that. How did you get out unobserved?'

'Pushed the bike across the chalk-pit and round the

sheds behind Ancrum's slipway, then through the bushes to the slant road. It's the way the children go.'

He opened his door and got out. 'How should I see through sheds and bushes when the C.I.D. failed? I didn't follow you. I came on my own account.'

He undid his tie and pulled it off, then slipped out of his jacket, which he dropped on the side of the car. He looked half dressed in the formal white shirt buttoned to the collar. The sleeves clung in creases to his arms. He opened the boot, took out a long piece of string, closed the lid and spread his jacket over it. 'Hold that,' he said.

I obeyed, neither understanding nor questioning. He went to the fence and pulled away my bike.

'What are you doing?' I said.

'I'll tie it to the back.'

He lifted the bicycle on the boot, fitting the handlebars over the drop of the occasional seat.

'I don't want to go yet,' I said.

'Where were you going just now?'

'To look round.' His eyes were not easy to meet; nor to avoid.

'How long have you been here?' he said.

'About fifteen minutes.'

'Why did you come?'

'I don't know.'

'Just fancied a run? I should have thought you'd exhausted the amenities of this place yesterday.'

'Why should you be the one who always asks?' I said, not very boldly. 'What brought you here?'

'Curiosity. I told you I suffer from it.'

'So do I, that's all.'

'Yours must be pretty powerful to push you twenty miles

up the hills on this old iron. And for someone professing a clear conscience you made a very cautious exit.' He began to fasten his tie round the handlebars.

'Please don't,' I said. 'I don't want to go.'

'I'll wait.'

Wait to see where I should go and what I should do.

'I'd rather you didn't,' I said.

He knotted the other end of the tie round the slam handle on the off side door. 'What's made me unsafe all of a sudden? You've relied on my tameness all summer.'

It was no worse than what he'd already said, yet somehow much more alarming. He threaded the string through the rim of the bike's back wheel and passed it round the rear fender. 'Agnes the supreme eater and haver of cake,' he went on, 'playing with fire and playing safe. Perhaps you can look after yourself better than I thought. I didn't give enough credit to your instinct for choosing partners who won't take advantage.' He pulled the string tight and tied it.

He was too serious. That was what had changed since he stood at the kitchen door launching truths and sarcasms from a base of tolerance and acceptance. These stabs were hard, sharp, almost wild; as if he'd been hurt himself, or frightened, or both.

He straightened up and leaned against the car. 'We've been swinging on the rope,' he said. 'It wasn't duty that kept us out of trouble, only caution. And for me the experience of twenty-odd years of falling off and getting hurt. Nowadays I stick by reflex to convention.'

'Except for Livia.'

Why did I have to say it? Why did I fail? I'd tried so hard to dismiss it as a random vicious kick.

'Who told you?' he said, after a minute.

'Sankton.'

'When?'

'This morning.'

'What did he say?'

He was turned away from me, with his hands resting on the side of the car. I repeated Sankton's callous casual sentence, omitting the reference to myself and to his grey hair.

He looked at me for a moment. 'I asked her. That's all.'

'All!'

'She said no, of course. Quite gently. No snubs. She has a sweet disposition, you know that.'

I remembered the Sunday afternoon; the polite child inclining her head, the brief smile, calm, unshocked, businesslike, her embarrassment when we'd met later on the Promenade, his hopeless look, the hesitation that evening in the door of The Ship where he was drinking, lonely, melancholy, disappointed, mortified.

'How could you think she'd say yes?' I said.

'Think! Who the hell thinks? If only one could. Afterwards, even five minutes afterwards, it's easy enough. Did *you* think, in that linen cupboard?'

'I don't preach twenty-odd years' experience.'

'I'm sorry. Let's leave it. She said no, that was that.' He hesitated. 'She told me there was someone else. Not that I didn't know already, or I shouldn't have asked.'

'You mean it adds interest to steal them away?'

'I mean I don't want the responsibility of being first.'

'So you assume no girl who comes from a broken home could possibly be a virgin at the advanced age of twenty-one.'

'Listen,' he said, 'you won't like it, but listen. I was up in Sankton's office waiting for change one afternoon when Livia came back from lunch. She'd been shopping and she dropped the basket. Virgins don't need some of the things she'd bought. Unless they're not intending to stay so.'

'Does that make her free to all comers?' My voice was trembling. 'Leave her the right to a private life.'

'You don't care for humans, do you?' he said. 'You just pay lip service to what you think is a grown-up attitude. You only love saints. And if you can't find them you'll make idols and blind yourself with your own incense.'

Livia. Olive-skinned satin-haired Livia. Only looks like that wiped out reason, memory, convention. Moderate claims of knees and arms and pretty mouse-hair could be resisted: a trifling inconvenience. The ones who wouldn't say no were the ones who wouldn't get asked.

'Come on, Agnes,' he said. 'I'm sorry. Shall we go?'

I looked at the bike tied to the back of the car. Sluggishly my mind returned to the picnic wood, the clearing, the Avon robbery.

'I must—stay a bit.'

'Curiosity killed the cat.'

'Have you satisfied yours?'

He nodded, fidgeting with the bike.

'How long have you been here?'

'Longer than you. Long enough.'

I looked at the flint wall. 'In there?'

'Yes.'

'Will it be dangerous for me to go in?'

'No. Pointless.'

'You went.'

'I was prepared.'

'For what?'

'For humans to be humans. Fallibility, the condition of error. There are no living saints, don't you understand?

Only men and women. The whole thing's founded on a fault. Male and female created He them, and then laid down the tables of the Law. The mess, Agnes, Agnes, the appalling mess.'

He turned to me with such distress, almost as if he were pleading. I didn't understand. I was tired after my toil up the hills. I didn't want to talk, even to think any more, I just wanted to finish whatever I'd come to do.

'Let me fall off the rope,' I said. 'I'll learn. You needn't wait. Take the bike off and leave it.'

He didn't answer; and after a moment I walked away, down the road towards the lodge.

I was a botanist, a member of all Tom's societies, seeking permission to search the grounds for *Hordelymus europaea*. A line of washing flapped behind the lodge; but no one opened the door, looked through the window, no dog barked as I passed, though my feet crunched on the grit of the drive. I walked on, outwardly steady, listening for the sound of a sports car starting. The grounds were tended but not cherished, the grass was cut but not rolled. Nothing was turned to advantage; there was no improvement. I heard the eighteenth century term and the critical aesthetic track of my mind, and was caught in the discomfort of self-awareness. I should never be free again. There was still no sound of Hedley's departure. I came in sight of the house.

It was Edwardian, red brick, red tiles, gables huddled at every possible angle, faintly institutional, perhaps on account of the bare-earth flower beds sparsely planted with bush roses, and the chintz curtains, all too similar, showing too much bare glass, like the windows in the orphanage. I still hadn't heard the car; perhaps I shouldn't in any case through the trees and the wall.

The front door porch had a tiled floor and green-glazed pedestal-pots of fern, Victorian rather than Edwardian, I thought; for I had to think something to keep myself walking. White wooden arrows pointed into the porch and along the path which branched from the carriage sweep to skirt the house; Office and Visitors.

Perhaps it's that kind of club. If it were, they wouldn't tell me so at the office, they would only say they were sorry they could not allow me to wander their woods in search of a barley-like grass, good afternoon. I turned along the path; a visitor, short-sighted, absent-minded, feminine, who had misunderstood the notice, seen only the one. I turned the corner of the house.

They had sunk the lawn, and set it out with croquet hoops. Two women with shining hair and large bottoms were playing, standing with their backs to me, one of them taking aim with the mallet. A few yards along the terrace were garden chairs and an iron table messy with crumbs and a disordered tea tray. From open French windows to my left carried the high china-clay voice of an English middle-class girl.

She was curled in an armchair beside the blind eye of a television screen. She was young, pretty; her delicate skin had never bent over the blast of an opened oven or the steam of a washing-up bowl. From her white Burne-Jones throat piped an insipid plaint.

'But what can you do? You're helpless, flat on the couch with not a stitch on, he's got you just where he wants you. The things he asks you to do! I'd no idea—'

She broke off because she'd seen me; but it was the one standing by the window who spoke.

'Hullo,' she said, 'are you the new recruit?'

'I'm a visitor.'

She grinned at me. 'Health? Or outer space?' She looked me quickly up and down. 'Planet Venus, I suppose?'

There had been a girl like that at Harefield; short, dumpy, with the face of a Cheshire cat, and wide bright eyes; a nymphomaniac, she'd been, fully attested.

'I come from Gunfleet,' I said. She was younger than me, twenty-three, perhaps twenty-four. In spite of the warmth she wore a long thick knitted cardigan; the pocket at the hip bulged with paper tissues.

'Gunfleet.' The languid voice dragged from the Burne-Jones throat, bored, unconcerned. 'I suppose it's about Livia, then.'

Livia. Hedley. Sankton. Avon.

'Yes,' I said, 'where is she?'

'That's the trouble, she's gone,' said the dumpy one. 'Left, skedaddled. She won't have had time to let you know, perhaps. She only went yesterday.'

Yesterday. The day of the picnic. 'Where?'

'Wouldn't they like to know!' She caught her breath for a sneeze and pulled at the tissues. 'You'd better go to the office,' she said, wiping her nose. 'They probably can't help you, but you could try.'

The Burne-Jones twitched a magazine off the television set. 'Malone might know.'

'I think she's on duty. I don't suppose they'd like you to talk to her. They'll show you the door pretty quickly. Would you like to, though? I'll take you to the annexe.'

'You'd better not,' the Burne-Jones said, without looking up from the magazine.

'Come on. I'll put you on the path, anyway.'

The dumpy figure stepped out of the windows. A croquet mallet clicked against the ball as she hurried me along the terrace.

'Malone's a lazy bitch,' she said. 'Livia used to take a lot of work off her hands when she didn't feel up to it. She's going to miss her. Of course I can tell you *why* Livia went. She wasn't happy. I've only been here a week and I could see she hated it. Most of them treated her like dirt. She used to say money wasn't everything. Let's go through the laurels, we shan't be seen.'

We went down six steps at the end of the terrace into a thick shrubbery. The girl sneezed again.

'Curse this bloody cold. They can't touch me while I've got it. I want to get back to work.'

I could see her stand at the bar in a circle of glasses and grinning men, indomitably turning each sally with a husky riposte. We passed a tennis court; its net sagged into the weeds.

'Malone may be rather cagey,' she went on. 'She let Livia take on too much, and that's made trouble as things have turned out. Wait a minute. Stand still. There's the big white chief.'

Through the trees I could see the end of the house. A man in a dark suit crossed the red brick and disappeared from sight.

'Temporary,' she said enigmatically. 'Has he got worries! He has to account for the geese and the golden eggs.' She turned to me. 'I think I'll beat it back to the nest. Keep straight on. You can't miss the annexe. Ask for Malone. She might give you an address. I know she used to post letters for Livia.' She grinned at me. 'Wish me luck.'

'Good luck,' I said mechanically. 'Thank you.'

She ran back the way we'd come.

Livia had left, skedaddled, yesterday, surprising them. Sankton had driven away on the London road. Livia, Sankton, Avon. I walked along the damp sun-mottled path.

I couldn't say, madam. She said she'd found a job with better pay. Flat on the couch with not a stitch on. The things he asks you to do. Perhaps it's that sort of club.

Hedley said that. Hedley knew the short cut to Dyer Street, had stayed overnight in London: so he said. But it wasn't only Hedley. Tom, Ian, Tubby. Three able lonely disappointed men, all short of money; earning as much as before, short therefore because they were spending more. Avon robbery! Those hours on the marsh, bird watching, working late, which had provoked in Hedley the castor oil smile that at last I understood: *cherchez la femme.*

Livia. Olive skin, satin hair, almond eyes, flawless living perfection. She'd beaten me hands down, on all counts. I'd never grudged her beauty. She hadn't even left me what she didn't want.

It was my own fault. *Cherchez la femme.* Agnes, the wife, drifting, duty-bound, rarely asked, never refusing but always longing for someone else, Agnes the spend-thrift, egoist, flirt. *Cherchez la femme.*

Livia. She wasn't happy. She hated it. Money wasn't everything. Livia was gentle to Hedley, she had a sweet disposition, she had come to me for lessons, Livia from the broken home.

There was the annexe, once cottages, for gardeners perhaps, now converted and extended. For what?

I didn't care for what. I'd neglected her. Wherever she'd gone, whatever she'd done, I'd find her and I'd help her. If she wanted it.

Yet I was afraid to go to the front of the annexe, coward,

I walked round the side of the extension, sheltered by lilac bushes. I had lost my bearings. In front of me, some yards through the shrubs, I saw the flint wall covered with ivy, and trees beyond. I heard voices.

They came from an open window that might have lit a lavatory, a narrow sash about eighteen inches wide, a few feet from my head. I moved close, pressed to the wall.

'Cover that, his nibs will want to see it.' A brisk female voice. 'Put it on the sill in the shade. Makes a change when they take us by surprise. Pity it had to be her, she's heartbroken. Still, that's life. At least there won't be a row about this. He can't blame Mother Nature.'

There was a small clink of metal on stone. By the window I saw a freckled arm and a breast under starched linen.

'It's his own fault anyway. He shouldn't have brought the stuff in.' A different voice, soft, suburban. 'I didn't know it existed. Mr Regent never uses it.'

'Mr Regent knows what's what. His nibs is full of foibles and fancies. All show. Come on.'

The arm moved away. On the tiled ledge inside the window something lay under a folded cloth. The soft voice spoke again, receding, the other answered. Silence. Suddenly I smelt something, hanging on the air their movement had disturbed; something so unexpected that I took a moment to identify it: surgical spirit.

I closed my eyes, pressed the back of my head against the wall. Jesus, I thought, forgive me, forgive me, all of you. My follies are so great they're a sin.

It wasn't a middle-class brothel. It was a private nursing home for wealthy snobs and she couldn't stand the patients. Livia had struggled to train as a nurse. I was answered, and all I had to do was slink away with my shame.

A blackbird flew out of a bush, scattering drops. One day years from now I would confess to Tubby: *when the nurse put a bedpan on the window ledge I woke up!* though the covered shape was too small for a bedpan. On an impulse I lifted the cloth.

Somewhere in the grounds a dog barked deeply, loudly, almost a bay. I put back the cloth and opened my mouth. The dog barked again, and I fled, straight to the wall, senseless, silent, panic-stricken, reached it, started to scale it, pulling on the ivy branches, hard as ropes. Life-giving rain had soaked them all morning and hadn't steamed out in the shade. I heaved, slipped, and caught instinctively at the top of the wall, packed with razor flakes, the stone man's weapons. I hung, scraped with my feet, scrambled back to the top, tearing stockings, knees, and hands, dropped on the far side and ran, tripping on brambles and the thousand snags of Nature, into the green ride, over the tyre marks, slipping on mud, slime, rain-moist earth, heaved at the gate and stumbled into the road, smarting with pain, opening my mouth to call out but crying unheard in a roar of exhaust, staggering towards the car that was going to leave; only it waited, stood with the door held open, a space, a goal which was all I could see, into which at last I dropped.

Movement took place round me, I recognized sounds, the door being slammed.

'Quick,' I said. 'Quick.'

'You're all right, Agnes. No one's going to hurt you.'

A strap tightened across my body. My hands were picked up and laid down again.

'Go on,' I shouted, meant to shout and whispered, 'go on, go on.'

Unfamiliar hands pressed my face and head. 'Agnes.

Agnes. Come on. Come on, lass. What did you see? What did you see then?'

Someone's responsibility, lying in blood in a kidney bowl; as long as my hand, slippery, purplish pink like a young skinned rabbit, with spindly close-cuddled arms, a top-heavy head, and a filmed currant for an eye: the due, the reckoning of the game, the outcome of beauty and romance, the issue of male and female. A foetus.

Chapter Ten

Tom stood above the armchair, which Hedley had pulled into the kitchen so that he could keep an eye on me no doubt. Mittens nuzzled in the crook of my arm.

'She was kneeling in the church for over an hour,' Hedley said, out of sight. 'Father Ryan saw her and it worried him. He came up to the cottage to see if you were at home and met me. We went back just in time to pick her up. She'd eaten nothing solid since yesterday afternoon, if you call a picnic solid.'

'What were you doing in the church? What's happened to your hands?'

I didn't speak. What good would it do?

'She was frightened,' said Hedley, 'that's why she went into the church, she's frightened now and she was frightened when she cut her hands.' He moved the double boiler on the cooker; he was making a custard. 'She climbed a flint wall at Lawne.'

Tom brushed his hand across his hair. 'I asked you not to go out,' he said. 'I asked you not to say anything, yet you must repeat what you've done—'

'She didn't have to tell me,' said Hedley. 'I went to Lawne myself.'

There was a quick tap at the door, and Tubby was in the room. He was light on his feet, the fat loafer. He stared for a moment at my hair.

'My God!' he said quietly, and turned to Tom. 'I saw the car go down the drive.' He hesitated, glancing at Hedley. 'Carole thought you'd want to know they've found Lenny.'

'Lenny?' Tom repeated absently.

Tubby came forward. He must have hurried along the street, he was sweating; but he wasn't out of breath, his face wasn't red.

'He'd gone right out to the old sheds by the paper mills. Poor chap. They've taken him away for questioning. That's what they always say, of course. I don't know how they think they're going to make him understand.'

He was trying desperately to get some message across to Tom, whose face remained a distracted blank.

'Tom's only just come in,' said Hedley. 'He hasn't had time to hear the local news. Except that Agnes and I went to Lawne this afternoon. Not together. We met at the ride that leads to the gate in the wall.'

'Agnes!' said Tom. 'Agnes, you didn't—'

'Wait a minute, wait!' Tubby shut the kitchen door. 'That's something. Now. Let's hear them, Tom. We needn't say a word.' He looked at Hedley. 'Come on, you're never shy, are you? Never slow to give tongue.'

It was stupid, unjust, untrue; and calculated.

Hedley tested the custard on the back of the spoon, poured it into a bowl and brought it to me. 'Shall I tell them?'

'My God, you play her like a plastic yo-yo, don't you?' said Tubby.

Mittens started to snout greedily round the bowl, though he had been fed. Hedley picked him out of my arms. 'Save your breath,' he said, without looking round. 'She went up to Lawne because of the Avon robbery.'

Their eyes turned on me, quite blank. I took the first spoonful of custard. It was smooth and not too sweet. He'd used yolks only. I suppose he was used to cooking for himself. He scraped the remains from the saucepan into the cat's plate, and rinsed the pan under the cold tap. Mittens was clinging to his shoulder. He lifted him down to the plate; and all the time his clipped voice was repeating what I'd told him, the pointers that had seemed to me so damning, so possible, that in fear and weakness I'd poured out as we came from the church to the cottage, locked like lovers because of my shaking legs, the suspicions he'd heard without comment, holding me steady across the back, with his arm that felt like a lagged metal pipe, the evidence that now sounded so callow and far-fetched. He told them everything; except the most important thing of all.

Mittens jumped into my lap, licking his chops, settled on my stomach and began to clean his face with his paws. I put down the empty bowl.

'Thank you for your compassionate interest in my debts, Agnes,' Tubby said slowly. 'As it happens I haven't any outstanding, but if I had I might have appreciated a loan of hard cash more than curiosity. Only sympathy costs nothing, I know. So you thought we were hard up. True. But if we planned to enrich ourselves from the Avon moneybags, why should Tom have sold the microscope and let the caravan? Why should we sell the binoculars and the camera—assuming we have?'

'You couldn't use your own car. I thought you'd have had to buy one.'

'I see. Invest in success. And what did you hope to find at

Lawne? A nice fat cache? No, you hadn't thought. You never think, I doubt if you can. Otherwise you'd have thought that Tom would hardly invite a friend of Walter's to live within fifty yards of him.'

'You could have wanted information from me,' said Hedley, 'bought or painlessly extracted. There must be plenty of details that even Tom wouldn't know and might find hard to learn.'

'Why Agnes went doesn't matter, nor even what she found, if anything.' Tubby looked at Hedley. 'Don't tell me those sage silver hairs cover such melodramatic grey matter! What took *you* to Lawne?'

'Curiosity.'

'I see. When you itch you scratch. What set you off?'

'Some of the things that sent Agnes,' he said, refusing the provocation. 'Not all, and not for the same reason. I went to Lawne because I wondered what was going on among you. The picnic was just the culmination. There were other things that Agnes didn't notice or didn't give any weight. Let's leave them till they come.'

He looked at me: the familiar level candid look. 'You said the owl pellets made a detective of you. You didn't mean it. You might pull scabs off people's lives by accident, but you wouldn't take pay to do it. I did. For twelve years I've been a private detective. Part of the scum that drifts round the divorce courts.'

I put my hand over my mouth, and immediately he turned away, thinking perhaps that I'd moved in disgust; whereas I was only stifling, for the worst time, the egoist's futile cry: I didn't mean it.

'Who's paying you?' said Tubby, suddenly quiet, even anxious. 'How long, and for what?'

'No one's paying me. I'm teaching myself Russian.'

'Why here of all places, Gunfleet?'

'Chance. It appealed because it was dead. Or seemed so. I thought I could isolate myself, make a break. I should have known better, myself and things in general. You can't dodge your lot, you become what you do.'

'You don't ask us to believe that?'

'I don't expect you to.'

A misspent life. I wanted to die. Ring out the old. I tried.

'It's true,' I said, 'if he says so.'

'Agnes, you're a credulous lemon,' said Tubby.

Hedley shrugged. 'If it troubles you, ring Walter. Perhaps you'll believe him.'

'He told us to ask no questions,' said Tom.

'He was only trying to save me from what he knew I wanted to drop. As if I could. You only had to mention Sankton pinching lead from the batteries and my curiosity woke up. I kept his sheds pretty well scanned. There was nothing you wouldn't expect, second-hand cars and spares and tyres and junk. Then of course that fellow was hanging about, the ex-Avon rogue, and I told myself there was no harm in passing that on to Walter, for what it was worth. It seemed so trivial at the time, I didn't bother till I'd seen him there myself. If I'd relied on Agnes and spoken sooner it might have spiked their guns. Because when I made the paper hats at the picnic I read the description of the car that was used for the robbery, and the number. And I'd seen it not so long before, standing in the back of Sankton's long shed.'

'Sankton?' I said. 'The robbery. Is that why—'

He nodded. 'I rang Walter at home yesterday evening. We knew the car would have gone. Sankton probably did no more than provide it, no questions asked. All the same Walter said he'd get his security round and tell the C.I.D. That's why I took my own car down to The Ship for the night, in case someone overturned a can and dropped a match in the excitement.'

'This might be mildly interesting at another time,' Tubby said, 'but the only connexion between us and the Avon robbery is in the enthusiasm of Agnes.'

'Don't underrate her,' said Hedley, 'and let me finish. Sankton must have been warned he was tabbed, or he saw it for himself. He'll have the same sensitivity to being watched as I have, from the other side. It's that sort of life. Perhaps he had other irons in the fire because evidently he decided to withdraw to some quiet retreat. Nothing so drastic as flying the country. The Sanktons don't get into dangerous trouble except by accident. But the Avon affair alone could put him inside for a spell.' He looked at me. 'When you met him in Shayle he was leaving. He wasn't stopped, because he was quick, but they took the car number. And then of course they had someone else to consider. Someone from Gunfleet, someone to whom he'd just said good-bye.'

I flushed, remembering Sankton's farewell.

'A woman,' he went on, 'the giver-away of secrets, the indiscreet, the weak link in any chain. They didn't know how far he was involved. He might have left you watching the till. Their job depends on taking long chances, not discounting the unlikely. Nothing is impossible. They wouldn't stop you. They'd rather see where you went. Especially after you'd changed your hair.'

'They?' said Tubby.

'The police. The C.I.D. Perhaps they knew her anyway. Tom's quite a prominent local figure, so is Ian, so are you.

I think I put them off when we drove home. Perhaps not. But they had someone at the end of the path by the time we were back.'

'My God,' Tubby said quietly.

'Surely they're not still there?' said Tom.

'No, they're not, because the police picked up Sankton on the Mediham by-pass. I rang Walter half an hour ago. He told me.'

'Then what does it matter?'

'Christ!' said Tubby, 'don't you see? They watched her when she went to Lawne on her bloody bicycle.'

'She went out the children's way,' said Hedley. 'They can't be everywhere. They haven't got limitless resources to spread on a couple of thousand snatched without bloodshed, not on so slight a chance. I don't think she was followed.'

Tom's face was white. 'Even if she were,' he said, 'they'd have no cause to do anything. It would have been unfortunate—they'd think, draw conclusions. But there was nothing wrong. Nothing illegal.'

Tubby sat down at the table and rubbed his face. 'Sorry about the barbs,' he muttered to Hedley. 'I might have known they'd bounce.'

'You wanted me to fly out in a fury and leave you alone to tell Tom.'

'What?' said Tom. 'Tell me what?'

Hedley looked at me, hesitating.

'Go on,' I said. I was surprised it came out, that I had breath. 'I know.'

He came and stood beside me. 'Lenny found a girl on the marsh this afternoon. Dead, stripped, dumped in a ditch.'

Tom looked up, frowning. He was deputy curator of Shayle Museum. It wasn't the milieu of violence.

'I went round the village looking for Agnes,' Hedley said. He put his hand on my shoulder. 'I heard what they were saying. She seems to have had an incomplete abortion.'

I pushed Mittens into Hedley's hands, stood up, and walked across the kitchen.

'Where are you going?' said Tubby.

I put my hand over my mouth and broke into a run, through the bathroom, slammed the lavatory door and bolted it. Probably they wouldn't doubt me, wouldn't bother to follow. I unlatched the bar of the window, pushed it back against the outside wall, put down the lid of the lavatory seat and stood on it. I'd often wondered whether it would be possible to climb out. It was quite easy, as my mind had grown suddenly to understand the word. I scraped my dried grazes, and bruised my arms, and twisted my ankle as I jumped down; but I was out. I ran down the path to the street.

They were still there, the old men and women. Their proper time had caught up with them, sundusted evening. Their eyes followed me, the single moving object, newly blonde, with laddered stockings and bloodsmeared dress, a bare-armed woman who only had to exist. Heads stared down from the keystones of the terrace porches: Victorian plaster women with crimped hair and dimpled chains and small modest mouths. I reached the Promenade, went round to the back of the house, tapped on the kitchen door.

Helen came in a second. She stared at me, stupefied.

'I want to see Ian,' I said.

She shook her head. 'You can't. He's busy.'

'Helen, it's important, urgent. I must. Where is he?'

She didn't take her eyes off my hair. 'You,' she said. 'You two—'

'I know. I know. Only not now, Helen, please, later, I'll explain everything. But I must see him. Please, please Helen.'

She nodded. 'In the darkroom. Be quiet.'

I ran across to the shed. The blackout curtain was drawn. I knocked, and opened the door.

He'd been writing at the table. He turned round. He had his glasses on; but I couldn't see the likeness, though I looked and tried.

'Agnes,' he said. I realized that he hadn't known me for a moment because of the hair.

'What is it?' he said. 'I'm terribly busy.'

His eyes didn't change, he didn't smile. He had a headache. I can't, I thought, I can't tell him now. Later. When his headache's better.

He was waiting for me to speak and go, too tired to be puzzled. My voice stuck in my throat. I held out my hand, and in his unfailing gentleness he took it. He looked down at the roughness of the plasters, and with a shudder snatched back his hand and turned away. It was the blood. He couldn't stand the blood.

Someone knocked at the open door. I looked round, expecting Helen, and saw Hedley.

'It's all right,' he said quickly. 'Tom and Tubby are coming. They went by the path in case you'd gone that way.'

'Get out,' said Ian.

Hedley stepped across the threshold. 'I've come to take her home.'

Ian turned to me. 'Why did you come, Agnes? What did you want?'

'Nothing,' I said. 'It'll wait.'

They watched each other with something I didn't understand; enmity, hatred, fear, none of them exactly, all at once, a whole beyond my knowledge. It sickened me, so that I nearly cried with relief when the others came to the door.

Tom pushed past me. 'Ian,' he said, 'do you know? Have you heard?'

Why did it have to be Tom who hedged and dreaded and asked what we all knew?

Ian looked at him. 'What do you mean?'

'He means Livia,' Hedley said, so quietly I couldn't believe it. 'Did you put her in the ditch?'

Ian sat down. 'Agnes, go home,' he said. 'You'll have to go alone.'

'You needn't be afraid of her,' said Hedley. 'She'd cut her own throat rather than let you be hurt. She knows.'

'Then she's no right to know,' Ian said in a low voice. 'No one had any right to tell her, and she's no right to hear more.'

'Wait a minute, Ian.' Tubby closed the door, just as he had thought to close the door of our kitchen. 'Nobody here had to be told by the others, at least as far as the main issue is concerned. Agnes found out for herself. We all know, and knowledge gives a right. You wanted my advice before, take it now. Tell us the truth.'

'Not in front of Agnes. She won't stand it.'

'She's stood the worst already, alone,' said Hedley.

Tom sighed. 'Let her stay, if she must.'

'I haven't got time,' Ian muttered, 'don't you understand?'

'Yes, we do,' Tubby said with sudden authority. 'We haven't much time either. Tell us.'

We were crowded together in the small shed under the light of a naked bulb stuck from a socket in the wall: hemming him in.

'I can't think,' he said wearily. 'You know so much. What more?'

'The beginning,' Hedley said.

Ian leaned back in the chair. 'She was sitting in one evening. I came back early, I had a headache. She made me tea. The next time I just came back. I only wanted to look at her, be with her. I didn't mean it to happen. But she was so—not just beautiful. I can't explain. Ordinary, human. I couldn't go on. All that sweetness—I hadn't realized how much I'd wanted.' He moved his hands helplessly, like a blind person. 'It didn't seem to matter to her that I was so much older. I don't know what pleased her so. And once it was started I couldn't go on without her. Like sleep. Can't you understand?'

I could understand. Ian with his charm and smile and delicacy, so far from the whistling drivers of the estuary, the love and protection she lacked. Livia with her flawless beauty and ordinary sweetness, the respite he craved.

'Go on, then,' said Hedley. 'You got her pregnant. Those Fridays, her afternoons off, when you were supposed to play golf with Tubby, when the landlady was safe behind the stocking counter. Weren't you afraid someone at Culham Park would see Tubby alone when he was supposed to be with you?'

'I never played alone,' Tubby murmured. 'I used to go along to Connell's. There's a room behind the billiards. They play—it doesn't matter. I used to make a bit, lose a bit.'

'And Ian went in by the side door in Dyer Street that isn't overlooked,' said Hedley. 'When did she tell you? Straight away?'

'We had to wait till the second month,' Ian said, halting. 'It was so difficult, we had to be so guarded. I tried to find excuses to get up to Sankton's, she tried to find me in the village alone.'

The paraffin can in the blaze of summer, the threshold of the pub, the reluctantly accepted lift in Helen's van. If I'd spoken to Livia she might have confided. I would have helped her. But I'd stayed with Hedley. My summer had been a mirror and key to what had happened, and a fever that blinded me to it. Ian, Livia, Hedley, me: only a razor edge of chance and hesitation divided us.

'She wouldn't write to her mother,' Ian went on in a low voice. 'She didn't want—I had to find somewhere. I asked Tubby.'

'I knew chaps at the hospital who'd know. There are quite a few places. It was a risk to take the one near Lawne, perhaps. Twenty miles isn't far. But the place is so secluded, and it's in everyone's interest to be quiet. It's legal, reasonable, quite good.'

'So you banded together to pay for Livia's abortion.'

'No,' said Tom.

'This place at Lawne isn't just for that,' Tubby explained. 'Sometimes there are dangers—well, always, to a certain extent, but I mean that would be present at term—weak hearts, blood pressure. Or the girl leaves it late. They can treat the place as a private nursing home, stay and have the baby in retirement. It's an ideal spot for middle-class girls. None of their friends are likely to be passing through to the estuary. Just at the brink of squalor and amenity. And that's what was planned.'

'How did she keep her mother from knowing she'd moved?' said Hedley. 'Did you pay the landlady to send on letters?'

Ian nodded. 'She wanted to keep the room in any case, to go back to. It was all she had. We had to pay for that, and extra—'

'To shut the woman's mouth. Did she know you, see you?'

'No. Livia arranged it all, the sending on of the letters.'

'Not to Lawne, surely?'

'To a cover address, with a false name.'

'Skinner's?'

'How do you know?'

'You went there—never mind. Why not Stenlock's? Or your bank?'

'I couldn't afford Stenlock, still less now. And the bank's ruled out because I was afraid—we have a joint account.'

'All right. Did you pay Skinner?'

'No. He's known us all our lives. He takes a lot in his stride.'

'So you collected the mother's forwarded letters and sent them on properly addressed to Livia at Lawne. And she wrote to you, under the same cover.'

Ian flinched. 'I had other people to protect. There are so many duties, so many ways you can do harm. In the end I didn't know what I was doing.'

Hedley stood looking at him, expressionless. 'What were you going to do about the child?'

'I'd thought of putting it for adoption. She didn't want to keep it.'

Hedley turned to Tubby. 'I suppose at this place you paid roughly the same either way. Why not abortion?'

'You can't do that,' Tom said, 'destroy life.'

'It's a crime,' said Ian.

'A crime. Suppose no one adopted the child, suppose it was passed from pillar to post—' He was silent a moment. 'And I thought you said the place was legal?'

'So it is, technically,' said Tubby. 'Everything fixed, their own doctors sign the chits. In any case that's not obligatory. I know people are encouraged to think it is, but in fact you're only *recommended* to have the second opinion if you're going to operate. After all, for a thousand quid you can get an abortion without anyone's blotting a line. And I mean from a chap with a brass plate the size of a cheval glass—oh, what does it matter? She wasn't to have one, that's all.'

'So you all paid up to let her carry the baby. Seven months of steep fees. And for anonymity you'd need hard cash. No wonder you were short.' He looked at Tubby. 'That Friday when we met in Culham. Had you been detained at the hospital?'

'No, I was an ornithologist trespassing all unwitting into the grounds at Lawne, vetting the place. I could get some idea at least what it was like. Ian was making arrangements with the girl. Tom went to London to sell the microscope.'

If I hadn't forced them to have tea they would never have met, Hedley might never have guessed. My vanity had precipitated his suspicion. My fault.

'So you sent her off alone?' said Hedley. 'You never visited, of course.'

'What else could I do?' Ian said with intensity. 'I've got a wife and child to think of, something you don't understand. I know, I know, I should have thought of them before. But I didn't.'

Think! who the hell thinks? Hedley had known when he spoke to me outside the wall, not all, not the worst, but enough. I understand that now; he was trying to prepare me, perhaps. If only they'd told me. I would have helped them. She wasn't happy there. Money wasn't everything. Livia, facing all those months alone, inescapably burdened with an unwanted child, gentle Livia who couldn't spell.

'She used to work with the nurses,' I said.

Tubby exclaimed softly. Ian looked at me with horror. I remembered that to him I was the outsider in the family; I had no right to know.

'You're not the only one who vetted the place,' said Hedley. 'Agnes did. I did, even more thoroughly. This afternoon, when we'd seen her landlady, and I'd begun to see the truth.'

If there had been no Avon robbery Sankton wouldn't have gone, the garage would have been open, someone would have sent the woman away before we arrived, he might never have suspected.

'I've come to the part I don't know,' he said. 'I *can* guess. Picnics, phone calls, nightjars, cars that coast by the caravan and appear scratched next morning—'

'Don't go so fast,' said Tubby.

'The picnic, then. Were you going to risk a visit?'

Ian slipped his hand under the bridge of his glasses. 'She wrote to me, she was unhappy. She didn't like the place. She wanted to have the same as the others were having and go away. I wrote that I'd come out on the Sunday if she could get down to the door in the wall. Tubby saw it when he scouted about, it opens from the inside with a bolt and latch. Not to take her away, to talk to her, persuade her—I don't know. So in spite of what Carole arranged we had to go to Lawne. I didn't want to disappoint her.'

'Well? You went in the wood, Tubby and Tom patrolled.'

'She didn't come. I waited as long as I could after Tubby whistled.'

'So on the way home Tubby rang up, anonymously I suppose, to find out if she was all right.'

Tubby sighed. 'I used the cover name. They were cagey, but in the end I got the superintendent to admit she'd gone.'

'Cagey. Not alarmed?'

'No. More annoyed. I thought up the nightjar business to give us an excuse to confer.'

'Lenny heard your phone ringing in the afternoon. It wasn't the nursing-home trying to get in touch?'

'I have a wife and family too,' said Tubby. 'It would have tied me up too much to give them my number.' He paused. 'Livia knew it. We'd arranged she could ring me if there was some personal urgency. Such as her mother suddenly writing she'd be home in a week.'

'Why not ring Ian? No, never mind.'

We all saw why not. At the office, the switchboard; at home, Helen. Whereas Carole would never bother, probably never notice, if a woman asked to speak to Tubby.

'She wouldn't have expected me to be out at Lawne too,' Tubby said. 'She might have rung. But why leave that very morning? Why not hang on a few hours till Ian came?'

'Can't you guess now?' said Hedley. 'She didn't want the baby. She helped the nurses. She'd trained for a time herself, she knew her way round. Remember I've seen this place. There's a temporary superintendent. Perhaps routine was slack—it won't be now. I think she had access to the medicine stores and she had to get out before they were checked.'

'But my dear chap,' Tubby said after a moment, 'I doubt if there would be anything she could usefully take. They work by surgery, much safer and more certain. They might keep some ergometrine for their few deliveries, it is sometimes given at term. But it's very uncertain in action. She could take a colossal dose and make herself thoroughly ill without necessarily producing the effect she wanted, she'd know that. I suppose you were thinking of ergometrine?'

'I'm not a doctor,' said Hedley.

His face had turned white, almost grey. They were all the same, even Tubby. And yet that was all there was to show for the frightful questions and answers. From the quiet monotony of their voices they might have been exchanging commonplaces.

'You pretended to go to Lindhurst, then,' Hedley went on.

'Tom and I did go. We'd said we would, and I thought we ought, in case it turned out afterwards the police had had blocks all round the area or something, and we couldn't have gone where we claimed.'

'Then you were expecting trouble?'

'We were in it already.'

'There were limits,' said Ian. 'I couldn't involve them more than I had.' He was silent a moment. 'I said I'd get back on the bus. I thought she'd go to the room, you see, I was sure. We were paying, she still had the key. I went round to the side. She'd put the ribbon over the curtain, the sign we had that it was clear to come in. She must have thought that when she didn't come to the gate I might guess—'

'At least she knew you'd come.' Hedley looked at me. He was thinking of my mother trusting Ian's father: the past repeating itself.

'The side door was unbolted,' Ian went on, speaking carefully, 'but she hadn't put up the snib on the kitchen lock. It didn't matter, I had a key. There was a risk that the woman would come in, but I remembered she'd been going on holiday and I was trying to work out the date. I went upstairs. Her door was open. I looked through the landing rail and saw her lying on the floor. I thought she'd fainted, I ran in.'

He stopped. I could hear his breathing, like the distant rasp of a saw.

'Well?' Tubby said suddenly. 'Go on. Was she dead then?'

I was trembling all over, it seemed, just in an instant, without warning. Ian didn't move.

'Tried to do it herself, I suppose,' Tubby went on. 'How? What did you find? What was she–'

'Don't,' I cried.

'Shut up,' Tubby said sharply. 'You wanted to stay. One's enough.'

I looked at Ian's ghastly face, and dimly sensed a purpose in what seemed brutality.

'What did she use?' Tubby repeated. 'You must have seen something.'

'A tube,' Ian said. 'Squeezed out, empty. A plunger fixed to the nozzle.'

'Pastes!' Tubby exclaimed. 'They hardly use them. Twelve, fifteen years ago, there was a vogue. How did she get hold of it?'

'The man,' I said. Tubby moved impatiently. 'The director, the temporary. He brought it there. It was his— idiosyncrasy.' The clumsy word fell heavily into their silence.

Tubby pulled himself back to the attack. 'All right. Paste then. Just as unpredictable, and awkward to use on oneself. The applicator has to go right up into the cervix. However it seems to have worked. How long dead, could you say? Was she stiff?'

Ian nodded.

'Can't tell anything,' Tubby went on: the dry bored relentless clinical voice. 'Say she did ring up in the afternoon, just before applying it. Her place isn't on the phone, she'd have to go out, rather a risk after. Two to three hours, more, less, for the stuff to work, it varies. She was in the bedroom. Not the lavatory?'

'Outside.'

'Even so—'

'She'd got it ready. A basin, a plastic mac, towels.'

Tubby let out a smothered groan. 'They will do it, think they can manage alone, it won't go wrong for them. The risk, the risk! even if they bring it off. Infection, gas gangrene even—'

He stopped, remembering perhaps that it wasn't *they*, but Livia.

'Of course there wasn't time for that,' he went on more slowly. 'You get vagal inhibition, air embolism. But the commonest cause is loss of blood. It can seep or it can come in a rush. Was there much?'

Ian leaned back in the chair. His hands lay on his knees, his eyes were closed. 'She'd fallen in it.'

Livia. Satin-haired Livia. Forgive me my share of blame, neglect, my selfish fault.

'It was my fault,' said Ian. 'I accept it. I didn't kill her, but I'm responsible for her death.'

Tubby sighed. 'The thing is, what's to be done now? We've got to know where we stand. What did you do?'

Ian put his head in his hands. 'It had to be cleared up. I found things in the drawers, pillowcases, more towels. It took—a long time.'

Ian. Ian who shuddered at a graze, swabbing the floods of an uterine haemorrhage.

'There was working out to be done, what would be right,' he went on stiltedly. 'There were other people to think of. Nothing could do her any harm. It seemed simplest if she disappeared. No one would know. The mother—but there wasn't so much love—'

'Never mind rights and wrongs,' Tubby said, quite gently. 'What we have to cope with is that you didn't carry it through.'

'It wasn't planned this way.' He hesitated, and sighed. 'It was so late it seemed safe to bank on the landlady's being still away. I came back on the bus. I had to have a car. I took Agnes's.'

Mine. The car in which a few hours later I'd sat the test. I felt only surprised, that he'd done it without my hearing.

'I knew the door of the cottage wouldn't be locked because Tom was out,' he said. 'I saw there was no light in the kitchen, and I knew the key was kept in the table drawer. I'm sorry Agnes. There was no time, I had to do what I could. I took the car out of the shed and let it roll down the slope. I wasn't used to its tight steering, I scraped the corner of the wall by the end of the alley. I drove back to Culham and parked it by the side door. I went in and bundled up her things.' He stopped for a moment. 'Her clothes—had to come off. I took them downstairs, those and the towels and the case she'd brought back, and put them in the boot. Then I wrapped her in the bedcover. There was still blood. I couldn't—do everything. I carried her down and put her in the back of the car.'

'Wait.' My voice was dry. 'Had you ever taken the car before?'

'Once. You were at the hairdresser's. Months ago, in the spring. I wanted to go there quickly and get back. There'd been a mistake, a muddle.'

'Where did you park it?'

'In the side road. There would have been no harm. If any one had seen they'd have thought it was you.'

'But I hadn't passed—'

'No one would have known, though. What does it matter now?'

'Nothing,' I said.

I understood. He'd wanted to be with Livia; he hadn't meant any harm, he just hadn't thought; he'd acted as I would have done.

Sankton had seen, noticed, hinted to me months later, written the address on the dirty receipt. *I tried to help you once before.* He thought it had been Tom, I suppose. That was his idea of help: the give-away. How had he come to see the car, to be there at all? Livia, Livia—no, Ian was right. What did it matter now? I brought my mind back to what he was saying, the deadly monotonous statement of accounts.

'I meant to go to the creek because of the current. I forgot the naturalists out on the marsh, listening to the migrations. That's where they were. I saw the reflectors of their cars as I came down the track. In a way it helped because no one would question mine, though they wouldn't I suppose in any case. There are often odd bird watchers. I thought I'd go back and wait, then that Tom would soon be home and miss the car. So I stopped where I was.'

The ditch by the side of the track; foul, stagnant, choked with moss. Livia.

'I put her in.' His voice was hardly more than a whisper, a voice at the end of its tether. 'I was going to put the clothes and towels on one of the fires, but I thought there was rain in the air, they might not burn, I brought them back. The car wasn't marked, except for the scratch. Agnes would think she'd done it herself, everyone else would, anyway. I drove up to the top and coasted it down the path, but I couldn't finish the turn into the shed. I had to get out and push it back the way it had been, facing the cottage. Then I came home. I meant to go back tonight, go on to the creek. Only Lenny must have noticed the break in the duckweed. It wouldn't have had time to close over. That's all.'

'So if Lenny hadn't chanced to go along that path we'd have I known nothing,' Hedley said, watching Ian. 'You'd have tipped her in the creek and gone home. All over. Forgotten. Carry on living.'

Tubby frowned. 'I don't see how you could hope—well, never mind, I suppose in the confusion—' He broke off. 'It hasn't turned out that way, has it? We've all got a share of the blame, the three of us, that is. Something to square with ourselves in private. Listen, Ian, it's detestable, but the girl did kill herself, after all. She'd trained for a time as a nurse, she must have known the risks. You did your best in the first place to put things right. You've got to go on. Explain. Tell the exact truth. There's nothing else you can do, after all, you can't get out of the country. It's a crime, concealing a death, a body, but it's not the worst crime of all.'

'Wait,' said Tom. His hands were shaking and he put them suddenly in his pockets. 'What good will that do? None to her and only harm to yourself and others. No one can connect you with it. Why should they? All the money transactions were in cash, there was complete anonymity.'

Hedley and Tubby made almost identical gestures of impatience. Even I could see gaping holes in the fabric of Tom's wishfulness.

'No use, Tom,' said Tubby. 'I've gambled all my life. If there were a chance I'd take it. Morally reprehensible, no doubt, but it would save a lot of suffering. There isn't a chance.'

'You can start with the home,' said Hedley. 'You say it has some pretensions to legality. Did they take her without an address? Somewhere to communicate in case of natural complications?'

'She was twenty-one,' said Tubby. 'She could have signed

her own operation forms if it had been necessary. They don't often bother about signing for anaesthetics, the ones they use for childbirth are so mild.' He paused. 'In fact they did have Skinner's address and the cover name. They told me when I rang up that they'd written to say she'd gone.'

'That's what you went to collect this morning?' Hedley asked Ian.

He nodded. 'Tom said he'd go at lunch. I couldn't wait.'

'Who gave them the name and address, Livia?'

'I wrote before she went in. I wanted to make sure things were settled—the way we'd decided.'

'It would have been a slow way to communicate in an emergency.'

'We thought of that,' said Tubby. 'They had a prearranged telegram, not too explanatory. Skinner could have phoned it to me.'

'Too bad if he was out.'

Tubby shrugged. 'She was healthy. We hadn't any reason to expect complications.'

'No one thinks of everything,' said Hedley. 'Your precautions were adequate provided nothing went wrong, but when it did you foundered on compromise. You tried to have it both ways, get out of trouble within the law, avoid a scandal and do your duty. I'm not condemning you, they're just facts. You couldn't bear to put her in some shady place that would take her money and ask no questions. You had to have the reasonable nursing home. And above all no truck with abortion, you made sure of that. There's all this writing and taking of addresses, partly caution, partly conscience. All traceable.' He looked at Tom. 'Don't delude yourself. The police have found her, they'll find the rest. They'll take her and they'll see how it was done, and they'll eliminate, starting with the obvious, hospitals, nursing homes, everywhere in the district likely to have held a tube of abortifacient paste. They know the place at Lawne, of course they do. They leave it alone, there's a law for the rich, even for the prosperous. But they know it, they'll go there. The *good* nursing home,' he said bitterly. 'So good they never thought to check the cupboards till twenty-four hours after a patient had gone. Or checked and covered up. The nurse covering laziness, the superintendent covering slackness, hanging on to their precarious legality, their dubiously clean record. It doesn't matter. Other staff, other patients, they'll be asked and they'll talk. Who she was, when she went, where she used to write. Someone will have taken letters to the post. They'll go to Skinner, then they'll come to you.'

'Skinner won't say,' said Tom.

'Then someone else will. Someone always knows and tells. Police stations swarm with busybodies passing on things they think the police should know, millions of words, day after day, malice or madness or genuine worry, sifted, classified, checked. One day, used.'

'You're not going to the police?' Tom said shakily.

'Why should I? There's no need.' He turned to Ian. 'I understand more than you give me credit for. Livia—you know, she told you, didn't she? Let it be, it's over. I know about the wife and child, I had those too, once. I've thought about you more than you know. I don't believe you could have hidden her body, thrown it away, forgotten, gone on living. I've heard the justifications you might have toyed with. I know the body was in the ditch, I believe it came there just as you said. You told the truth. Part of the truth.' He moved slightly, so that he stood by the window. 'I saw you turn green when I cut my hand that time. An inch, a little slit, on a man, a stranger. I can't believe you cleared up Livia's blood and cut off her clothes. You'd have had to, you can't pull them off when—after a time. If you'd killed her I could believe it, perhaps. But even now you can hardly bear the idea, the memory. How could you think, let alone plan? Or drive a car, however erratically? Besides, it would have been noisy and slow to carry her downstairs and get her into the back of a two-door car, difficult if not impossible. Unless you had help. And you did, didn't you?' He pulled aside the blackout curtain and looked into the dusky garden. 'Someone practical, strong, used to driving, someone whose stomach isn't easily turned, who could take charge in your utter incapacity, someone you had to tell, someone you'd injured, yet in a way weren't sorry to involve, to repay all the strains and restrictions that had driven you into the whole thing. And yet, after all, someone it's your duty to shield.'

He dropped the curtain. There were voices outside the shed, footsteps on the path. He leaned forward and spoke quickly. 'It happened the way you said, all of it. But you didn't plan it. You were there, taking the orders, like the dogged volunteer at Cassino.'

The door opened. Helen stood outside.

'Carole's asking for you,' she said shortly to Tubby. 'Someone rang up from the hospital.' She puffed out her red cheeks. 'This place is like an oven. Why don't you open the window?' She walked across and twitched back the curtain. 'Carole tells me they've identified the body.'

There was a little pause.

'They're local police,' Hedley said. 'They'll have seen her often enough as they passed on the road.'

She stood with her hand on the window bar; then without opening it she turned round, frowning at our faces, and finally, with the contempt she had always reserved for me, at Ian. Her mouth tightened in routine exasperation grotesquely inadequate to the circumstances.

'What *is* the use?' she said: her voice was the same brisk instrument as ever. 'You get me to cope with the situation, then ruin everything. You've told them, haven't you? What good will that do?'

He didn't answer, didn't move.

'I suppose you think I enjoyed it?' she said. 'It had to be done, that's all. It's typical—people make fools of themselves and expect someone else to clear up the mess. Anyway, it probably wasn't even yours.'

A vein throbbed in her weathered neck. Helen, who crushed the wasp without a qualm, because it had to be done. A stocky bulging figure in a bargain print, devoid of grace, charm, or love. *Cherchez la femme.* And yet it didn't seem enough. Who was to blame? What cause? How far did I have to strip back life and heredity just to find one small answer?

'Come on, Agnes,' said Hedley, 'I'll take you home.'

Ian sat with his head in his hands. I was nothing to him. I had no right. And if I had it would make no difference now. No one could help him, no one could console.

'Come on,' Hedley insisted gently. 'There's nothing you can do.'

There never was. I went through the door into the evening air, across the garden, into the drive, avoiding the street, taking the long way back to the cottage. He walked beside me but we didn't speak. I was already sleeping as I walked, feeling nothing, empty-headed, except for a narrow limited vision, a goal; a little cat and a silent bed in a darkened room.

I woke. Ancrum's whistle was sounding. There was a smell of coffee in the room. Sun streamed through the birches by the window. Their leaves were already turning yellow, flickering in the breeze that billowed the curtains.

I remembered.

I sat up in bed, hurting my hands as I moved, seeing without surprise that Tom's side wasn't disturbed. I pushed back the clothes and stood up, staggered by the aching stiffness of my muscles. A strange image moved in the dressing-table glass; a woman, myself, blonded in thoughtless vanity to further a summer flirtation.

I pulled on my dressing-gown. I had to go on. Last night I'd thought there was nothing to be done, but it wasn't so simple. Whatever happened he was going to need money. I'd have to go out to teach, get rid of the car—

It checked me. The car. I didn't want to think, but it was too late to stop; and I realized that this was the first trial of what life was going to be: a constant braking at the sharp bends of memory.

I put on my glasses and my watch. It was twenty-past ten. I saw from the frayed cotton of the sleeve seam that my dressing-gown was inside out. I ran the comb through my hair. She'd set it well, she always did. My face in the mirror was pale and slightly shadowed, showing up the freckles that missed Ian but came out in Malcolm. There must be a likeness, other people saw it. Surely he wouldn't deny me the right to help?

I glanced round for Mittens, but he must have run out. I

went downstairs, through the living-room. He wasn't there. He'd be in the kitchen, pigging away at his plate.

Hedley was pouring coffee: three cups. Tom sat at the table, as Ian had done, with his head in his hands. I should have to help him too, perform what was his right and my duty, comfort, console, sustain; and hope he would never know how little I felt.

'I was going to bring it up,' Hedley said. 'I didn't think you'd wake.'

He gave me one of the cups across the table and nodded at a chair. 'Come on,' he said, touching Tom's shoulder. 'Here's Agnes.'

Tom shook his head without looking up. 'Tell her,' he said indistinctly. I couldn't be sure, but I guessed from Hedley's face protesting against the weakness I'd come to accept as part of my lot.

'It's all right.' I sat down, because I thought I knew what he had to say. I hadn't expected them to have come so quickly. They would have taken Ian before I had time to see him; and I'd left him last night without a single word.

Hedley came and stood beside me; the stranger, the summer flirtation, faded, grey, furrowed, in a tattered khaki shirt and ancient trousers. I hadn't flirted for a long time now: and he wasn't a stranger.

I forced myself to swallow the coffee he'd troubled to make, looking over to Mittens' feeding plate. He wasn't there.

'It's all right,' I repeated. 'You want to tell me the police have taken Ian.'

He took away the half-finished cup. 'There's no nice way of telling you,' he said abruptly. 'I don't know how to soften what can't be softened.'

He picked up my hands for a moment, then laid them down; perhaps he was afraid of hurting the cuts. 'Ian's dead, Agnes. He and Malcolm. Helen went up at half-past eight and found them. It was sleeping tablets. He had a month's prescription.'

He held my shoulder. I heard the clock ticking, Ancrum's whistle sounding the end of the break, and down in the street the banging doors of Woodey's delivery van; and I opened my mouth to say *Where's Mittens?* as I looked without hope at the empty basket.

Chapter Eleven

The afternoon was thickening to its early dusk when he knocked on the kitchen door. I wiped my hands on my apron. I'd been peeling the potatoes.

'I'm going, Agnes,' he said. 'Come to say good-bye.'

He was wearing his navy-blue donkey coat. The car stood in the puddles of the path, its white paint spattered with mud. There had been rain all week, the second in November. The trees were almost bare, lashed by gales off the river.

'Take me up to the top,' I said.

'You'll only have to walk down again.'

'Please.'

'Put on a coat, then. It's cold.'

I took my old gaberdine from the hook by the door and followed him out to the car. He didn't have much luggage; it would all go in the boot. There was nothing on the spare seat but a book and his shiny black mac.

He drove down the path into the street, past the terraces and cottages, the dank gardens where a few roses lingered, buds that rotted without opening. By the closed doors of The Ship he turned into the drive. The ground was slipping under the wheels and I couldn't think what to say. We passed the hole, dark and unfenced, where the frayed rope hung from the bough. Lights were on at the pumps in Sankton's garage. I caught a glimpse of the new man's ginger hair.

He swung the car into the Roman road, towards Culham, the way he'd have taken me to London, if we'd ever gone; and when we'd passed the bus stop he pulled into the verge. There were one or two cars on the road and a couple of cement lorries. He brought out his cigarettes.

'What will you do?' I said.

'Go back. Go on.' He leaned on the wheel, bending over his lighter. 'And you?'

'The same, I suppose.'

'But you'll move to Shayle?'

'Perhaps. It isn't fixed.'

It would never be fixed. The longer we stayed, the more Tom would forget, buried, oblivious, drugged in work and the marsh. Already he was patching the breaks in his life. Tubby was going, Carole had insisted. She'd packed and removed the children straight away, taken them off with the pets to live with her parents. Lenny had gone, two weeks back. His mother couldn't stand the gossip, the baseless things that were said and looked; even when everyone knew or guessed what had happened, still they stared and hinted, doubted the safety of Lenny, the scapegoat on whom they unloaded their shock. So they'd gone, a family uprooted, no one knew where. And Helen, of course, had gone.

'Why did he leave Helen?' I said. 'It wasn't that he didn't have enough.'

'Helen wouldn't have taken it. She'd have known what he

was doing. Perhaps it was his obscure notion of private justice. Leaving her to take the measure of her responsibility.'

'But Malcolm.'

'God knows. He didn't want him to suffer, inherit the mess, the sins of the fathers, the past that was bound to come out. Pasts always do, charitable neighbours dig them up from the ends of the earth. Whether he lived or died himself, Malcolm would suffer. Perhaps he didn't want him left to Helen. Or he wanted to finish their stock, disgusted with himself or her, or both. There are so many things you can rattle off, glib, facile, separate. Whereas the reality couldn't have been thought at all, only confusion, disorientation. How can you say whether it was strength or weakness, duty or evasion, pity or vanity? Nothing is simple. There is no answer. Only people who'll tell you they've got one.'

'Don't hate him,' I said. 'Please don't go away hating him.'

He shook his head. 'He was the one that did the hating.'

'He didn't really. It was because of—'

Livia. Why had I ever thought it was on my account? She'd told Ian about Hedley, as she'd told Sankton. Sankton who knew her address, who'd seen the car in Dyer Street.

'Sankton. He was going to her house on her afternoon off, when there'd been a muddle, when Ian wasn't expected—'

'No,' he said quietly. 'Not Sankton. He was fast but he was careful. He knew how far he could go and when. Think for yourself. Remembering. Anyone might walk or drive along Dyer Street. I did, often. Futile, childish if you like. I haven't grown up, that's all. Perhaps Sankton hadn't either, in that respect.'

'She told Sankton—quite a lot.'

'She was young and alone and had no one to confide in. He was her employer. For all his faults he wasn't unfair to women, you know it. I think he treated her well.' The blue eyes looked at me steadily. 'You don't have to sleep with someone to tell them your private life. Do you?'

I had no answer to that, as he knew.

'Let her keep her fidelity, Agnes. One last wisp of incense.'

He wanted to keep it for her. And after all, what did it matter? Livia, poor Livia, with no one to confide in. I might have helped her. But it was too late.

He looked at my head. 'Your hair's growing out. There's half an inch of mouse at the roots.'

I nodded.

'You'll be all right,' he said. 'You've got your mother's grit.'

'Come back and see me,' I said. 'Write.'

He stubbed out his cigarette. 'What about?'

Hedley. Hedley who stayed through the long two months, dealt and wrote and warded off the inquisitive, sold my car for me, shopped, fed us, nursed us through; my conscience, my rock, my strength, who had driven me into the vet's with Mittens in my lap, my little soft-pawed pet, though he was already dead where the fox had got him.

'What do you think I'll have to tell you?' he said. 'All the news from the divorce courts you despise? Dear Agnes, today the scum is up to my eyebrows.'

'I'll never understand you, Hedley, never. But I don't despise you.'

'You might. You wouldn't stay dazzled for ever by your own whitewash.' He smiled faintly. 'Sometimes you make me believe in it myself.'

We'd given each other something then, in our summer; I a dollop of whitewash, he a handful of grit.

'I got quite encouraged,' he went on quietly. 'Something you suggested.' He hesitated. 'I wrote to her. You know.'

I knew. The blonde heartbreak, the one who'd said no. To her there was something to write about.

'What did she say?'

'I only sent it yesterday.'

I opened the door. I'd stood so much, I couldn't start snivelling now.

'I shan't write,' he said abruptly.

I got out of the car and shut the door. 'Send me a Christmas card. You needn't sign it, just initials.' Despair wrenched at me. 'Otherwise how can I know you're even alive?'

He started the car. 'You can look me up in the telephone directory.'

Hedley, Hedley! There are scalpels and there are flint axes. His face had turned white. I knew why: shock, alarm, fear of a difficult scene, unpredictable trouble. I'd failed at the very end, faced him with the seriousness that I'd denied, that was more than either of us had bargained for. Now he would run like hell.

'Smile,' I said. 'Go on. Please. Give us the core, mate.'

I looked down at his lined face and light grey hair, as I'd looked down months before in Ian's office on that cold summer day when he'd first worn the donkey coat; and after a moment he smiled, as he'd smiled then. I knew him better now, but he was the same; a candid blue-eyed savage, a man. And I was the same feminine sucker, the absolute nit of the bunch. There was still nothing I wouldn't do for him, absolutely nothing: even this.

'Don't worry,' I said. 'I shan't let you down.'

'Thanks, Ag.'

He drove away. He didn't even say good-bye. He'd gone, up the rise in the Roman road and over the hill.

Thanks, Ag. That was what Ian used to say, Ian torn apart and killed by the weakness and duty we shared from our father, Ian the brother I'd loved, idolized, absolutely adored as only Hedley knew. And Hedley was gone. I'd never see him again. He'd send no card. There are no consolation prizes. I could look for his name in the directory: but there are so many H. Nicholsons.

I didn't stand long on the verge; it was cold, the nights were drawing in. The road was empty even of lorries and Avon tanks. Good-bye, my love, I thought, good-bye, good luck. She'll be a double-dyed bitch if she says no twice.

I walked towards the drive. A line of mist lay along the river. The lights on the distant shore were moist and yellow. Sluggish plumes rolled from the cement works' chimneys and diverged, widening against the ragged sunset, darkening Gunfleet with their shadow. Gunfleet. Chalk-dust and water, where life, of a sort, would go on.

I glanced at my watch. It was late, later than I'd thought, twenty-past five. I had to get Tom his tea.

Mystery in the Channel
by Freeman Wills Crofts

Mystery in White
by J. Jefferson Farjeon

Portrait of a Murderer
by Anne Meredith

Santa Klaus Murder
by Mavis Doriel Hay

Secret of High Eldersham
by Miles Burton

Serpents in Eden
edited by Martin Edwards

Silent Nights
edited by Martin Edwards

Smallbone Deceased
by Michael Gilbert

Sussex Downs Murder
by John Bude

Thirteen Guests
by J. Jefferson Farjeon

Weekend at Thrackley
by Alan Melville

Z Murders
by J. Jefferson Farjeon

Praise for the British Library Crime Classics

"Carr is at the top of his game in this taut whodunit... The British Library Crime Classics series has unearthed another worthy golden age puzzle."

—*Publishers Weekly*, STARRED Review, for *The Lost Gallows*

"A wonderful rediscovery."

—*Booklist*, STARRED Review, for *The Sussex Downs Murder*

"First-rate mystery and an engrossing view into a vanished world."

—*Booklist*, STARRED Review, for *Death of an Airman*

"A cunningly concocted locked-room mystery, a staple of Golden Age detective fiction."

—*Booklist*, STARRED Review, for *Murder of a Lady*

"The book is both utterly of its time and utterly ahead of it."

—*New York Times Book Review* for *The Notting Hill Mystery*

"As with the best of such compilations, readers of classic mysteries will relish discovering unfamiliar authors, along with old favorites such as Arthur Conan Doyle and G.K. Chesterton."

—*Publishers Weekly*, STARRED Review, for *Continental Crimes*

"In this imaginative anthology, Edwards—president of Britain's Detection Club—has gathered together overlooked criminous gems."

—*Washington Post* for *Crimson Snow*

"The degree of suspense Crofts achieves by showing the growing obsession and planning is worthy of Hitchcock. Another first-rate reissue from the British Library Crime Classics series."

—*Booklist*, STARRED Review, for *The 12.30 from Croydon*

"Not only is this a first-rate puzzler, but Crofts's outrage over the financial firm's betrayal of the public trust should resonate with today's readers."

—*Booklist*, STARRED Review, for *Mystery in the Channel*

"This reissue exemplifies the mission of the British Library Crime Classics series in making an outstanding and original mystery accessible to a modern audience."

—*Publishers Weekly*, STARRED Review, for *Excellent Intentions*

"A book to delight every puzzle-suspense enthusiast"

—*New York Times* for *The Colour of Murder*

"Edwards's outstanding third winter-themed anthology showcases 11 uniformly clever and entertaining stories, mostly from lesser known authors, providing further evidence of the editor's expertise...This entry in the British Library Crime Classics series will be a welcome holiday gift for fans of the golden age of detection."

—*Publishers Weekly*, STARRED Review,
for *The Christmas Card Crime and Other Stories*